# The Revival of Molly O'Toole

# Praise for Robert Pacilio

## Praise for *It Was Never About the Books*

"If you ever had a teacher who changed your life, you're going to love this book. Robert Pacilio, an accomplished author and an award-winning teacher in San Diego, uses rock 'n' roll lyrics and films to help students unlock the power and mystery of literature. In his latest book, *It Was Never About the Books*, he shares vignettes of students who touched his heart, and whose paths he, in turn, changed inexorably. The book is full of compelling anecdotes, which lead the reader into the heart and soul of what it means to be a teacher. From encouraging an awkward student to find his confidence; or helping a neglected young girl feel seen and heard so that she can begin to believe in her own worth. This book will make your heart grow."

—SALLY FOSTER, DEAN MIRACOSTA COLLEGE

## Praise for *Whitewash*

"Whitewash is a slow-burn kind of novel, one that allows the reader to take in and really consider the issues at hand. With all the controversy and outbursts one expects in a courtroom drama, we follow the case through the eyes of Tony Rossi, a former high-school teacher, and we meet his fellow jurors and get to understand how they will eventually decide the fate of the defendant. I was very much a thirteenth juror as I read this book, struggling between my own ideals and the need to make a fair and just decision. A thought-provoking and enjoyable read."

—MICHELLE LOVI, ODYSSEY PUBLISHING, NEW ZEALAND

## Praise for *Meet Me at Moonlight Beach*

Robert Pacilio's *Meet Me at Moonlight Beach* is not a romance novel, but there is a lot of love in it. *Meet Me at Moonlight Beach* is about finding the love story you deserve long after you have given up on happy endings. It has been almost a decade since he retired from teaching, but Pacilio's second chapter has an awful lot in common with his first. He still believes in the power of words. He still loves a good redemption arc. And once he's said his piece, he hopes his audience understands a little bit more about themselves and the world around them, and that they will learn to love what they see.

—KARLA PETERSON, COLUMNIST, SAN DIEGO UNION TRIBUNE

## Praise for *The Restoration*

"Robert Pacilio's aptly named third book, *The Restoration*, does as it says. Set in the romance of the Art Deco styled Village Theater on historical Coronado Island, its characters emerge from the devastation of loss and the hopelessness left by the Vietnam War to new beginnings, unexpectedly. The warmth of the Southern California sun and the strength of the human spirit make it a nourishing and satisfying read."

—SANDRA GONNERMAN, FORMER SAN DIEGO COUNTY/HUMBOLDT COUNTY SCHOOLS LIBRARIAN, RETIRED

## Praise for *Meetings at the Metaphor Café*

"Oft-quoted American scholar and eternal optimist, William Arthur Ward once said, 'The mediocre teacher tells. The good teacher explains. The superior teacher demonstrates. The great teacher inspires.' We have found in *Meetings at the Metaphor Café* a great teacher, Mr. Buscotti. The descriptions of Mr. B's and Ms. Anderson's curriculum is enough to make anyone want to go back to school, re-read old favorites like *To Kill A Mockingbird* or at the very least, listen to some Bruce Springsteen! Every student deserves at least one teacher like this; a teacher who is passionate about the world we live in and determined to light a fire in each child. Robert Pacilio's debut novel rings with authenticity. This book is a must for anyone looking for a little meaning and a lot of inspiration, whether you are a new teacher or a lifelong student."

—BABETTE DAVIDSON, CEO OF PROGRAMMING FOR PUBLIC TELEVISION –PBS

"If you are an English teacher--particularly American literature--you would want to read this novel right along with your students. *Meetings at the Metaphor Café will* challenge the minds and hearts of teenagers everywhere"

—BRUCE GEVIRTZMAN, AUTHOR OF AN INTIMATE UNDERSTANDING OF AMERICA'S TEENAGERS

"*Meetings at the Metaphor Cafe* reads like an invitation...an invitation to sit down amongst its characters and relive your youth. With the turn of every page, you are transported back to a time when the world was new to you, sitting among friends, sipping a latte, discussing love and the meaning of things, and discovering life all over again like it was the first time. As a teacher, I can say that this book is a MUST read for any high school English or history class. *Meetings at the*

*Metaphor Cafe* should be in the hands of every teenager in America, and those of anyone who once was one!"

—DANIELLE GALLUCCIO, TRINITY MONTESSORI SCHOOL, ADOLESCENT ACADEMY DIRECTOR

"I thoroughly enjoyed this book. Robert Pacilio inspires the reader to be a better person and gives us faith in our new generation of youth. The take-home messages, however, engage a much wider audience and offer life lessons that build resilience and encourage a positive outlook on life, encouraging both youth and adults to make a difference in our society. This book is a must read for students, educators, and all the people who believe in positive change."

—MICHELE EINSPAR, DIRECTOR, TRANSFORMATIVE INQUIRY DESIGN FOR EFFECTIVE SCHOOLS

## Praise for Midnight Comes to the Metaphor Café

"*Midnight Comes to the Metaphor Cafe* is a testament to the possibilities of great teaching and the bounty in mind and spirit it can generate in young people."

—MARK MCWILLIAMS, MICHIGAN SPECIAL NEEDS ADVOCATE AND LAW PROFESSOR

# The Revival of Molly O'Toole

Robert Pacilio

The Revival of Molly O'Toole
Robert Pacilio

Copyright © Robert Pacilio LLC, 2025. All rights reserved. No part of this publication may be reproduced in any form or by any means without prior written permission from the author.

ISBN: 9798264680625

This is a work of fiction. All the characters and events portrayed in the novel are either products of the author's imagination or are used fictitiously, with the exception of the actual settings in Encinitas and Little Italy, California.

Editing, cover design, and pre-publishing assistance by Katharine Valentino. Author photo by Robert Bjorkquist. Cover production Robert Chisholm.

Robert Pacilio may be contacted through his website at http://www.robertpacilio.com.

# Other Works by Robert Pacilio

## Nonfiction

It Was Never About the Books

## Novels

Whitewash
Meet Me at Moonlight Beach
The Restoration
Midnight Comes to the Metaphor Café
Meetings at the Metaphor Café

## Plays

Whitewash (a readers' theatre)
Seventeen

## Poems

"La Petite Café at Midnight New Year's Eve": Creative Communications Top Ten Poems by American Teachers

*Dedicated to Linda Englund*

*She has demonstrated the courage and determination to prove F. Scott Fitzgerald wrong: There are "second acts in American lives." Hers is equal to her distinguished first act. Bravo.*

# Act 1:
# The Departure

## Act 1, Scene 1:
# Musso and Franks

"I quit."

"You ... what?"

"You heard me, Leo. I am quitting."

"Quitting...." Leo reaches for his water glass. "Quitting what?"

"Oh, for God's sake, Leo. You know damn well what. I am done with acting. Done, Leo. Finished. Drop the curtain." Molly flips her menu over from steak and chicken to cocktails. "God, I need a drink."

Leo's face morphs from shock to forced gaiety. "Whatever you order, you better make it a double because you are being ridiculous. You can't quit, Molly. You're just hitting a rough patch. Not even that, it's more like a slight ... bump in the road."

Molly signals for the waiter hovering nearby.

"Ah, yes, Madame. What would you care to drink?" The waiter's Spanish accent is refined. He is impeccably groomed, as befits the veteran staff at Old Hollywood's famous Musso and Franks. The Pantages Theater is just down Hollywood Boulevard, where *Hamilton* is making its West Coast premiere.

"I need to stay sober, and so do you. No doubles," says Molly to Leo. And to the waiter: "Sergio, I'd like a chardonnay ... or the house white, or whatever, just ... thank you."

"Of course, Miss O'Toole. And for you, Mr. Graborkawitz? The usual, I assume?" Sergio has served Molly and Leo lunch once every season for the last 20 years.

Leo waves him off with a brisk, "Yes. Yes. Sergio. An old-fashioned. Thank you." He removes his black-framed glasses, which he told Molly years ago he was sure made him resemble director Martin Scorsese. Once removed, his red-rimmed brown eyes diminish and age him.

Sergio observes the tension between his two regulars and exits quietly stage left.

Molly readjusts her posture, sitting straight now, and flips her grayish hair back so its red highlights glint. Her silver necklace has shifted and needs to be centered on a forest green blouse she selected specifically for this confrontation. She moves her clutch purse several inches away and places her cell phone beneath it. Nothing is to interrupt this conversation.

"I've had it, Leo. I am not playing the game anymore. I have been at it since I was ... I don't even know how long. We've been together ..."

"1989," Leo cuts in. He leans back in his chair. He has heard this before, so his rebuttal is practiced. "You and I came up together. You were one of my first clients. Forty years, and now, now of all times, you want to quit? Are you serious? I was just going to tell you about an audition ..."

Molly slashes right through Leo's charm and nonchalance. "Leo, do you have any idea how little we have accomplished in the last ten years? Sure, we've come up from the bottom, but you know what? The money you've made lately is from your other clients. I am still an extra on the call list, Leo. I am still on the *damn* call list."

She leans forward, "And no, I do not want to hear about the next audition because I know what that will be." She lowers her voice and glances around the restaurant. "It'll be another freakin' commercial for some goddamn prescription drug that nobody can afford, or even worse, a voiceover for the new Medicare supplemental insurance. Don't you get me started!"

Molly sits herself straight again and commits herself to her original plan to remain composed and committed. She *will not* reveal to Leo what finally broke her. Even though the pain and anger have been reduced to a lump in her throat, she will not, cannot, utter even one word to him about that.

The drinks arrive, and there is a short truce. Sergio has been a witness to similar scenes countless times: an actor and an agent in turmoil. In this particular revival, it is the aging, once lovely actress and her somewhat trusty, somewhat less influential agent trying to come to terms with the fact that both have seen better days. So often, this scene ends badly.

He gracefully places their drinks before them and has the sense to depart without asking what they would like for lunch. One never knows if there will be an appetite in the aftermath of such negotiations.

They sip. And breathe.

"Leo, listen to me. Just shut up and listen, okay? Promise for once in your life not to interrupt me. Just this once. I know I have been—we have been—at this juncture many times, but this time is different. This month I turn 60!"

"No!"

"What did I just tell you? Don't you say a word!"

She continues, "Look at me. I can't afford to keep coloring my hair, nor do I want to. I used to be a redhead. Now, red is retreating, and iron gray is on the march. That's my reality. This cannot be reversed. I don't want and can't afford Botox. I am tired of starving myself like I have been doing for three decades. I can't run or jump, and Pilates is a reminder that nothing moves like it should. Don't even talk to me about my sex life because I can't remember when I last got laid. My best days are long gone, Leo."

She falls back into the booth's plush cushion and lets out a sigh. "My first husband is a ghost, and my second husband's cheating and our divorce settlement—that you helped me with, thank you very much—has kept me in my home and prevented me from making a return to the can-I-take-your-order-sir-world." Molly tips her wine glass toward Leo and offers a toast to a successful divorce and four decades of a somewhat successful actor-agent relationship.

"To us," they harmonize.

Leo smiles, reluctantly, and sips his Old Fashioned. He has heard all this many times before from Molly, but she's never been this strident. He wonders out loud, "Molly, I hope this isn't out of desperation or hopelessness." His calling card touts that he is "The Agent to the Stars." He boasts that he deals with Hollywood's brightest stars, and he is trying to formulate another rebuttal despite the nagging truth—all their best cards were played decades ago.

Miss O'Toole is taking her last curtain call, and he is the lone member of her audience.

Molly refuses to shed a tear. She is far too Irish. With a final flourish, she swallows her wine and her pride in one movement. "I am *not* hopeless and I'm *not* losing my mind!"

Molly deposits the empty wine glass on the starched white tablecloth. She sighs and delivers her final line, "I'm not, Leo. But my father is."

## Act 1, Scene 2:
# The Amtrak Surfliner

"Callie, yes, the train is on time. I should be there in two hours. Right, I'm in the L.A. train station heading to Solana Beach, yes. Then we will go see Dad. Yeah."

Molly looks to see if anyone is gathering around the closed doors to the Amtrak Surfliner. She knows it will be a scramble to sit in a seat facing south. She hates the feeling of going backward in one of the seats facing north, though today, ironically, going backward seems fitting. She shakes off that thought. She reminds herself: *You are moving forward. Don't doubt yourself.*

Seeing that there's no competition for seats yet, she realizes she's hungry. "No, Callie, you're not cooking. I'm taking you and Tom to dinner, remember? No, no. It's my treat. Yes, I told Leo I quit. Yes! I did! No, I'm not kidding. I'm done. I'll tell you more when we meet.... What did Leo say? You know him, Callie. He tried to convince me not to retire. His usual bullshit. Look, I'd rather tell you about it when I see you. Oh, the doors just opened. I'm hopping on. I'll see you soon. Love you. Bye."

Molly boards, heads to the top deck, and makes sure she is facing forward on the side that will eventually give her a view of the ocean. It will take an hour to actually see the Pacific, but when she reaches Dana Point, the view will be lovely.

She used to make this trip routinely when she was at UCLA in the '80s and later as she was starting her acting career. Back then, she visited her family and friends on breaks, catching the train from Los Angeles's Grand Central Train Station for the two-and-a-half-hour ride down the coast to her hometown of Encinitas, an hour south of Dana Point.

Friends she met in California were envious that she had grown up in a beach town and always wanted to know if she was a surfer (she wasn't). However, the East Coast theater crowd she worked with later, during her time in New York City, just didn't get California. They heard the name "Encinitas" and assumed she lived in Mexico. All they knew about L.A. was that it was where television shows are born. Their distaste for her, her town, and the television version of their industry had been evident.

They usually made dumb remarks about how *genuine* art—that is, the theater—is created only in New York. But of course, they changed their tune once they landed a part in a television pilot. Hypocrites!

Molly interrupted her unpleasant memories of the past to focus on her worries about the future. How much can I get for my decrepit old house in Hollywood? How can I possibly afford something in San Diego? What will I have left for retirement ... as if I had the faintest clue what *retirement* means to an out-of-work actress?

She was about to embark on a journey, a long journey. She was jobless and, because of that, abandoned by her circle of always busy friends in the Los Angeles acting scene. Sure, they'd keep in touch for a while. One or two of them might even zip down to San Diego, once, if they could take time out from a desperate quest to find the role of their wilting dreams. Some of her friends had never given up hope that a film director might just turn them into an indie star.

They will be on call, she thought, just as she had been for the last four decades. A star on Hollywood Boulevard beats any promise of "getting together."

She understands. She has been the guilty party herself, losing friends along the way in the hustle and bustle to grab her moment in the spotlight. That's the name of the game. You have got to be in the right place at the right time.

But the right time has passed for Molly O'Toole.

The train is now rumbling past the ugly back lots of businesses that customers never see, with graffiti sprawled across all available cinderblock walls. Molly can't help but think back to those heady, innocent days when she would close a show or be done with a shoot and would race home on the train to tell her parents all the news of what it's like to be in showbiz.

Her parents would pick her up at the Solana Beach train station. She would hustle up the long cement ramp and hug her mom, who would help wheel her luggage to the family's latest used car. Her dad would be in the driver's seat, waiting at the curb. He'd jump out of the car and effortlessly toss the overstuffed baggage into the trunk, and then squeeze her so hard she'd have to brace herself to protect her ribs.

God, it was heaven back then.

Once her parents picked her up from the station, they would skirt the coastline to her favorite Mexican restaurant, Los Osos, and she'd order her Baja fish taco with rice and beans and sip a watered-down margarita, all the while talking a mile a minute about the latest famous star she may have met—or at least chanced to glimpse.

Her mother, Mary, was transfixed, eyes wide open, while her father listened politely, focused on how much the "no-business-like-show business" world might damage his red-haired miracle child. Liam O'Toole's never-ending river of fears formed a waterfall of worries: Is she too thin, likely from starving herself? Is she too tired from not getting enough sleep? Is she being taken advantage of—in more ways than he wished to ponder? Is she too struck by her stars to see straight?

"Oh, Daddy," Molly murmurs. "If you had only known back then."

Molly never spoke to them about the darkness that surrounds a career that weighs on a woman's soul. She never admitted that she bartered her soul for an audience's fickle attention.

While home, though, she did confide in Callie. Her twin sister could be trusted not to reveal too much to her parents about the backstabbing, the lecherous men trying to grope her behind the curtain, and the spiteful women with their claws out to warn her to "Stay away from my spot in line!" Callie was the only person she could also tell about the allure of drugs and wild parties and the undertow that pulled at her between love and lust.

She felt at ease to be on her way now to Callie and maybe, finally, on her way to being her own person rather than an imposter ... or worse, a poser. Loyalty had never been held in high regard in Hollywood unless the challenger had special status, either earned the hard way through grit and talent or, more often, acquired by birthright, money, or sex. Now, she might learn how to be loyal to herself. Trust had always been conditional; now she could start trusting herself to do what is right.

And love? Love had been her naïve sentiment for so long that it had become a pretense. Pretending, after all, is what actors do for a living. Actors play their parts.

But the lure of love, oh, there was the trap.

Teddy had been Molly's first love.

Teddy had performed for Molly the moment she was cast beside him in the play *Plaza Suite*. She played Mimsey, the bride who would not come out of the bathroom on her wedding day, regardless of her parents' pleas. Not until the climax of the play when her fiancé, played by Teddy, called her. And then, voila, out she popped, lovely, radiant, and oh-so-confident that this was the man of her dreams.

The two of them were not on stage until the play's third act. They spent much of Acts I and II backstage, locked in young love's embrace. In the darkness, they were alight with lust. They composed themselves, often just barely in time, for their entrances on the stage. Molly, flushed and quite aware of her red-faced countenance, reasoned that perhaps Mimsey was a blushing bride after all.

Ah, to be young and in love.

It was a comedy. Cue the curtain call, and all's well that ends well ... until it didn't.

The Amtrak Surfliner brakes screech, rousing Molly from her past and reminding her that her present drama is by no means a comedy.

## Act 1, Scene 3:
# Callie and the Pannikin

"Watch your step, folks," the train conductor booms.

Molly steps off lightly, carrying her overnight bag. She can see her sister joyfully waving. It seems that no matter the occasion, Callie always looks as though she is waving *bon voyage* from atop the bridge of a cruise ship. Her exuberance is endearing, even though the cause for it is amiss.

Molly notices that the Solana Beach train station seems frozen in time. Train stations never seem to change. The corrugated steel half dome atop this station looks like it was built during WWII and resembles the backdrop for the play *South Pacific*. The clock that sits atop the station has never worked, at least not in Molly's memory. It is perpetually stuck at midnight. Or high noon. Who knows?

The twins embrace and kiss. "I'm parked just down the street. We have time to grab a bite at the Pannikin. Sound good?" Callie knows the Pannikin Cafe is Molly's favorite. The two of them have a long history with the nostalgic cafe.

Across the busy, buzzing historic Highway 101, the sunshine-yellow Pannikin Coffee House stands as another memento of times gone by. Built in 1887 to accommodate the Southern Railroad Company, it was the original train station that dropped folks off in downtown Encinitas. Molly remembers her father saying it was initially painted fire truck red.

Molly's father often regaled the sisters with the history of the Pannikin. Over their hot chocolates, the sisters would listen to their father between his sips of coffee.

"In '69, they closed her down, but someone bought the train station and paid a fortune to lift 'er up and drop 'er down right here on the 101 because that way cars could stop for a cup of coffee and a cinnamon roll—like the one you two just devoured. Trains were outta fashion then." He would then wipe whipped cream off Callie's nose.

Years later, it became a tradition for the sisters to go there for coffee in the days when drinking coffee made them feel like real adults. Now, Callie and Molly sip their café lattes and pull apart their shared cinnamon roll. Molly sizes up the changes she observes in Callie, whose curly strawberry-blonde hair has now almost disappeared, replaced by a shiny light gray.

"God, I love this place, Callie. I remember all the times we would come here after school or practice. We'd talk about the boys we hated ... and loved. And sometimes we'd find Dad here when he'd finished a job, and he'd tell us not to blab to Mom about him getting a slice of pie. Remember?"

"Oh, yeah, I do. He always loved the banana cream pie. Yep. And he'd let us finish it so we would all be guilty." They both laugh so hard that Callie snorts. With that, they burst out laughing louder.

When they finally compose themselves, Molly says, "Callie, you look so relaxed since you retired. And I can tell you've kept on losing weight. I'm so proud of you. I was here, what ... two months ago? Every time I see you, you look healthier."

"Thanks. I'm glad it's noticeable. I've been working on it. I had to, Molly. Teaching all those years was just a lifestyle that didn't work for my figure. You know how it goes. The first ten years, you gain five pounds. Then you get pregnant, and there are five more. You repeat that, and a couple more pounds get attached. Before you know it, you've been teaching for thirty years, and you have thirty pounds to lose. I feel so much better. Mentally, too."

Callie stops picking at the pastry between them. "All that sitting. Eating as fast as you can in the lunchroom. Exhausted from the day and willing to eat just about anything me or Tom could throw together for dinner. It all added up."

Molly now feels guilty for ordering the pastry. "Wait. How long have you been retired now?"

Callie finishes her latte. "This is year three. And I've dropped half—fifteen pounds just because I have less stress, more rest, and we both are eating better. Tom has lost a little, too. But he never really gained too much. His metabolism. My maternalism. Whatever. It's just harder when you are older."

"Do you miss teaching?" Molly pushes the plate with the remaining pieces to the far edge of the table.

"I miss the kids. I miss their joy and energy. But that's about it. I dunno, Molly. Teaching was such a drain. Now, Tom and I talk about missing our own kids. How empty the house seems." Callie pauses to consider telling Molly what else she *really* notices. "Well, I guess, I also miss being so important to my students and their families. It is an adjustment no longer having that purpose each day."

Molly nods. The adrenaline rush of the audience, the encouragement from a film crew on a TV shoot, lights, camera, action! All that has kept her feeling alive and engaged. She knows exactly how Callie feels. But her sister walked away from her profession on her own terms and with a lifetime pension. Although Tom and Callie's kids are out on their own, the kids are their legacy. When the cameras stopped rolling, who was there for her? *Who, indeed?*

They sit quietly for a few minutes taking in the change in both their lives. Molly thinks about the colossal effort to lift that old train station from its roots and painstakingly deposit it on this piece of the highway. The Pannikin Café's revival. A new coat of paint and people who come for companionship. *Is that all it takes?*

Molly shakes the thought as if trying to clear her head from a bewildered dream. "How is Dad? At Christmas, I knew he was faltering a bit mentally. But then, when we had lunch with him two months ago, he seemed to be lost more than I expected."

"I think Dad has something in common with you, Molly. You are both good actors. He was trying to put up a good front then. But it's been, what, seven months since he moved into memory care, and every time I see him, he starts out very disoriented. Then he seems to catch himself and ... well, I don't know. He is moving much slower. His doctor says that some patients can stay at a plateau for a long time. Others, not so much. You'll have to judge for yourself."

Liam and Mary O'Toole had prepared for old age. They had downsized to a one-story home that would accommodate all their necessary possessions. The rest they gave to charity. The girls could still visit and share a bed, like they did as kids, in the guest bedroom. Liam spent extra for a queen bed that was needed only for three Christmases when the sisters stayed over for a night.

Growing up, they had boyfriends or parties or theater events to lure them away from home. Liam and Mary just accepted their fate and waited for the day when grandchildren finally came crawling across their living room rug. It took longer than expected, but Callie and Tom finally had two little ones in back-to-back years. Molly married, but her acting career had never given her the opportunity to have children.

They had aged gracefully until their good fortune had run out eight years ago. Liam always thought he would be the first to leave this earth. He was four years older and carried scars from decades in construction.

Mary's life, meanwhile, was not quite as physically demanding but far more stressful. She was a nurse. Night shifts. Double shifts. Emergencies. Being on call. Taking care of everyone except herself. When Liam urged her to retire, she ignored him.

Then one morning, she never got out of bed.

Liam found her. He crumpled to the floor. "Not her, Dear Lord. Not her."

## Act 1, Scene 4:
## Liam O'Toole

From the parking lot, Molly always gets the impression that the senior care facility is a fashionable hotel with well-manicured grounds. When she enters the lobby, she's always aware of the upscale ambiance of a Hilton or a Hyatt, and that visual extends to the formal sitting room with a fireplace and the adjacent dining hall. The décor is bright and seasonal with summer blossoms and the subtle, delicate musical stylings of a piano echoing throughout.

As Callie punches in the code to enter the memory care wing for assisted living, the homey atmosphere transforms into a necessarily antiseptic and utilitarian setting. As much as Molly wants to ignore the dramatic difference, she can't help but sense the ominous nature of this wing of the facility. It is, after all, adult day care with nurses, caregivers, and an occasional doctor roaming the halls.

Liam O'Toole has been here for three years, but he was moved to memory care just before the holidays last year.

He has his own room for now because he maintains enough cognitive and physical strength to show his independence. But just barely. His doctor told Callie that he has recently begun to wander the halls and doesn't always know where he is. If this becomes more commonplace, he will not be trusted to be alone.

Liam always told the girls when he first agreed to be a part of what he called "the senior club" that he didn't need "no damn special care." He barked, "Hell, I can feed myself, and I remember everything and everyone!" He thought that being in memory care was "for the birds."

On his good days, when he was first assigned to memory care, Liam would linger near the door—he called it the "escape hatch"—waiting for someone to leave, and then he would either slip behind them or stick his foot out as a doorstop. His caregivers would eventually find "the Rascal" in the restaurant grinning widely and devouring an ice cream sundae. "Great 24-hour service here, ain't that a kick in the pants!" he would say with a wink and a smile.

Those days are over. His resolve to "beat the system" as well as to fight his deterioration is waning. They know—he once knew, as well—that it is just a matter of time before the darkness will devour his mind.

During Christmas, one of the nurses told the sisters that the entire staff loved Liam and that "the Rascal" never acted mean or ill-spirited. That was a relief; Alzheimer's disease often brings out the worst in people.

Molly knocks on her father's door. When she opens it, the full impact of their father's prognosis presents itself. Liam appears to be talking to Mary. He doesn't even realize his daughters have come into the room.

"I tell ya, Mary. These ballplayers today don't hold a candle to the guys that played in the old days. See that guy? He points to what he apparently believes is a television on the near wall. Sandy Koufax would have put him away in three pitches. Three! All these kids do is swing for the fences. They never ..."

Callie touches his arm. "Dad. Dad, it's me and Molly. We're here to visit with you."

"Hi, Daddy." Molly sits in front of his lounge chair and touches his hands.

Liam looks at the girls, bewildered for a few seconds, but then he glances to his left where he apparently believes Mary sits in the opposite chair. Callie notices this and quickly takes the place of her mother.

Silence. Liam looks back and forth at his two daughters. Then he gathers his wits about him. "Oh. Oh. Geeze, girls. I thought you were the nurses. How stupid of me. I just got confused. You caught me off guard. Gosh. I was watching that damn ballgame." He then wraps his arm around Callie and squeezes. As soon as he lets go, Molly scoots up to him and hugs him.

"Oh my God. You girls look ... look so grown up. I mean, look at you two. My little twins are ... Mary, aren't they lovely women? Where has the time gone?" His eyes water.

Callie usually visits at least once a week, and by now knows what to expect. Molly, on the other hand, has to do all she can not to burst into tears. She turns away so he can't see her face.

Callie says, "Dad, you are the one who looks so g-good. Did you dress up special for our visit today? Tom would say you look *sharp*."

"Oh, Oh, yes. As a matter of fact, I told the nurse, you know ... what's her name? ... wait, don't tell me ... ah ha! Bonnie! That's the one. She helped me pick out this getup." He is wearing his favorite green flannel shirt and black corduroy pants. He smiles and then looks over at Molly. "You okay, kiddo?"

Molly recovers quickly, as a trained actor must, and replies, "Oh, Dad. Of course, I'm fine. Fine. I love that you're growing a beard. It reminds me of when we were kids and you always grew a winter beard."

"Well, it's Christmas and I thought what the heck. It's all white now, so when the grandkids come over, they'll think I'm Santa. When will they come to visit?"

Callie goes along with his assumption that it's Christmas and that her children are still young enough to believe in

Santa. "Oh, yes. Well, they're visiting Tom's parents today. They'll see you soon. Probably tomorrow."

"Oh, that's fine. Fine...." Suddenly, he seems lost. The agitation and energy he displayed just a moment ago have dissipated. It's as if someone pulled a plug, and his circuits just froze.

The sisters fuss over him. They ask if he's cold. He isn't. Does he want a blanket? He does. Has he been drinking his energy drink? That's what they call it; it's really Ensure, which the nurses give him to try to keep his weight up. His belt is loose even though it's fastened in the tightest notch.

Soon, they both realize that he's nodded off. They make him comfortable and lean his chair back.

Molly tries to process his transformation. It's only been a matter of months. Callie steps outside to let his nurse know he's asleep.

Molly kneels next to him and kisses his cheek while she wipes her tears away. It's no use. There is no stopping it.

## Act 1, Scene 5:
# A Scene in an Italian Restaurant

"*Buonasera*! Callie and Tom. It is so nice to see you again, my friends. And you bring me a guest. Ah! Who is this lovely woman?"

Carlo, his usual effusive Italian self, is dressed in a color-challenged red and purple striped long-sleeve shirt and black leather skin-tight pants. His hair is receding but remains curly and is unnaturally and suspiciously jet-black.

Carlo is Carmen's husband. Her name adorns their cozy Milanese bistro, with two Vespas parked near the entrance. Carlo is both the proprietor and entertainer. However, the kitchen is off-limits to him because that is Carmen's domain.

Callie introduces the "lovely" guest, Molly.

"It's so nice to meet you, Carlo. Tom and Callie keep telling me about your wonderful cuisine. I'm excited to be here."

Carlo bows and receives Molly as if she were royalty. This is his custom whenever he is introduced to a beautiful woman.

Molly is familiar with the Italian affect, a hearty serving of gregariousness and genuine affection. Italians sashay through life and embrace every minute. She has scrutinized actors in Hollywood, trying to imitate the Italian allure, but very few of them are actually successful. With Carlo, however, this is no act.

"It is my pleasure, *Signora.*" He signals to Carmen much like a Carabinieri in the middle of a chaotic intersection. "Come here, please. Carmen. Look here. Come. Come! Meet our new guest."

Carmen immediately comes from her kitchen, wiping her hands on her apron and giving a look to her cooks to discourage them from continuing their culinary bickering, normally part of the ambiance of the bistro.

Carmen embraces Callie with a lightning-quick hug and pivots over to Molly, touching her elbow. "Oh, *Piacere!* Carlo, make sure they have the quiet table in the corner." She makes eye contact with Molly, "So nice you have come. I come back and talk with you later. Busy! Busy tonight!"

She bows her head and pivots back to her kitchen, from where they can hear her commanding one of the cooks to listen to her and stop whatever he's apparently doing incorrectly. Molly, Callie and Tom all grin.

"Please. Please. *Andiamo!*" With a flourish, Carlo seats the ladies and makes a show of presenting them with the menu. "I'll be back in a minute, so you can consider what I can get you to drink." He pirouettes to the next group of guests who enter stage left.

As they nestle into their seats and place their crisp white table linens on their laps, Molly whispers to Tom. "Oh my! He is a character!"

"Oh, he's that way whenever we meet him, even outside of his restaurant. We shared a table with him and Carmen at an art festival fundraiser. He is literally the life of the party."

Callie bends closer to her sister. "They came from Milan twenty years ago and worked in other restaurants until they had enough confidence and funds to open their own place. Carmen is the nuts and bolts of the team, but she is self-conscious about her English. Once you know her, Molly, she's so warm and down-to-earth."

Callie puts her menu down, and her voice drops even further. "During the pandemic, people in town made sure they stayed afloat, and the patrons paid extra, some as much as a couple hundred dollars. We chipped in what we could, too. They remain so grateful." Callie turns her menu to the next page, and Tom peruses the wine list.

"White or red?" Tom asks Molly.

"Oh, a bottle of red, most definitely."

Tom and Carlo chat about which Chianti, Carlo assuring him that the Super Tuscan wine is delicious, while Molly takes in the scene.

The décor is modern and minimalist. No garish plastic grape vines or posters of The Godfather, no generic family photos cluttering up the walls in a tacky attempt to manufacture Italian ancestry. The colors are black and white with a splash of red. Elegant, not pretentious. Carlo delivers all the bursts of color necessary.

After wine has been decanted and sipped and bread has been broken and dipped in olive oil, the sisters brief Tom about their father, after which all three settle into a discussion that could be titled "What's next for Molly O'Toole?"

Molly launches into an explanation for her decision to quit acting. "You've heard my stories over the years. When I started out, a producer or casting director had his hands all over me because I was young and 'oh-so-pretty'." She pauses to take a sip of wine. "Guys, you do realize that the Harvey Weinstein headlines are just the tip of the iceberg?"

The salads arrive and Carlo asks, "Is everything *perfetto*? Let me know when you have decided on entrees ... no rush ... no rush. *Aspettare!* You need more bread and olive oil, too. Right away." He spins back to the kitchen like a whirling dervish.

"God, I love bread!" Molly smiles. "It is such a relief to allow myself to just eat and not worry about every freaking pound." She dips the crust into the olive oil. "Okay, where was I?"

Tom reminds her. "Harvey Weinstein ..."

"Well, long story short. You've heard all this many times."

Callie nods while nibbling on her salad. "Many times, but I love hearing about all the shows and the actors and actresses you got to meet in your glamorous years."

"So, anyway, you guys know when I was married to Kurt back in the '90s, things in the industry were busy. That's when I had recurring roles on a couple of shows, and I felt that my life and my career were going just fine. The money was good. Kurt was advancing at Pixar studios, and so I'm 32 years old and hitting my prime."

Another sip of wine.

"When Disney bought out Pixar, Kurt cashed in, and naturally, by the way, that was when I discovered he was cheating on me—remember, that was the first time ... and the second time with his 'assistant.' That's when I was done with his bullshit. So anyway, that began the slog through the divorce settlement that eventually allowed me to get the house. That's one reason I can retire now, because I got the house, and I have both a pension from Actors Equity and a nice nest egg from the divorce. Believe me, Kurt had a windfall from the Disney acquisition, and some of my share in the divorce was in stocks ... is this? Wait, this is turning into the long version of what is supposed to be the short story."

"No. That's okay, Molly," Tom says. "Remember, I came into the O'Toole world in '94 when Callie and I got married. By then, you were, in my mind, a big star." Tom has devoured his salad and is soaking up the dressing with bread.

"God, was it in ... hold on ... you guys are coming up on your 30th anniversary in August. Oh, my God! What have you planned? Are you having a party or just a quiet romantic getaway?"

Callie reaches across the table to put her hand on Tom's. "The romantic getaway. We're driving up to Santa Barbara for some wine tasting and fine dining. We haven't been there in years."

"Oh, you guys are still the cute couple. I love that you have never lost that spark."

Carlo has topped off Molly's wine as well as Tom's. He asks about their entrees and agrees to their choices of Lasagne alla Bolognese and Costoletta alla Milanese. "*Delizioso!*"

Tom hands the menus to Carlo and cuts to the latest in Molly's drama. "What did Leo say to you when you told him you quit?"

Molly assumes that Tom's question suggests that a counter-reaction by her manager could ricochet on her, cutting her off from her world and the connections she has nurtured.

She leans into his concern. "Tom, Callie knows just how crazy this job is—I use the term 'job' loosely. It can just take your soul." Callie nods.

"Leo knows it's a buyer's market, and a 60-year-old actress like me is a dime a dozen. He knows that whatever opportunity I ever had to keep the spotlight on me has passed. I suppose he feels a bit guilty that every time I was close to that spotlight"—she sighs— "the focus just slipped away to some younger, sexier, blonder woman. Who the hell knows why? But the point is, Leo's going to have to just let me go. I can't stay stuck in this ridiculous industry any longer."

"Was there something that happened, Molly, that ... I don't know ... broke you?" Callie asks.

"That depends. That goddam depends." Molly knows that the specifics shouldn't be discussed during a lovely Italian dinner. At least not now. So, she covers for herself and only admits to the superficial reasons. "It's never one thing. It's the landslide of rejections, or maybe a better way to say it is that my work became so trivial ... so commercial. Guys, if I have to do one more voice-over for a kitchen cleaning product or a feminine maxi-pad...." She shakes her head.

"Oh, I *thought* that was your voice, for Stay Free Maxi-Pads." Callie realizes this is not the time to be supportive of Molly's work. "Sorry."

"Geeze. Was the money worth it?" Tom's sensible nature comes into play. Once an accountant, always an accountant.

"Tom. Seriously. Are you asking me that?"

"Well, I was just wondering ..."

"No, it was not worth it, Tom! I can't believe you think that, as an actor, I can feel any self-worth shilling for crap like that. And the money sucks, too. God, if I was a big star like Tom Sellick, I'd be doing freaking reverse mortgage commercials. At least then I'd be on camera—probably selling my soul."

A pause in the action. All three players freeze. No one wants the temperature to rise any more than it has.

"Guys, I know the rags-to-riches romantic illusion exists in everything ... every story of stardom or fame. But the honest-to-God truth is the same old song. It's who you know, who you're related to, who you slept with, and who's your daddy and how much money does he have? Me, I had nothin' but a degree, a dream, and a desire." Her voice cracks and trails off. "Excuse me. Sorry. I didn't want to get emotional."

She reaches into her purse for a tissue and places it carefully under her eyes to make sure her mascara stays on perfectly. The rest of the story will come when she has a better grip on herself. She takes a deep breath to release the tension that has been building ever since she said the words *I quit.*

Timing is everything. Carlo returns with their entrees, lightening the mood with his banter about the efforts he and Carmen take in sourcing the finest ingredients to serve his special guests. He places the dishes before them with elegance and panache. Tom orders another bottle of wine.

Molly looks Carlo in the eye. She knows he's been discreetly eavesdropping, and she sees the compassion he has for a fellow dreamer. They nod to each other.

They dine.

Only when the entrees are finished and Tom tips the last of the wine into each glass does Molly raise the question, "How about splitting a dessert?"

The tiramisu is delicious, but Callie only takes the tiniest sliver. Molly mirrors her sister's willpower to support her, and Tom happily gobbles most of it. Coffee comes with the treat. It allows each of them to wash away the end of a career.

"So, I guess, the next thing for me to do is start looking for a place to live here in San Diego."

Before either Callie or Tom can reply, an interloper joins the party.

## Act 1, Scene 6:
# Alan and Zoey

"Oh, my God, Dad. The sauce smells delicious. Fighting the five o'clock traffic up the freeway from downtown is murder, but your cooking makes it worth it." Alan's daughter, Zoey, drops her satchel from her shoulder and reaches for the red wine and a glass.

"And how was Paris?" Alan Bernstein stirs the red sauce that has been simmering, marinating with sweet Italian sausage and pork knuckle. It's a family recipe, which Sophie carefully trained him to prepare in her absence decades ago when she had to work extended shifts at the hospital. She wanted some real food when she finally escaped from the bedpans and bloodwork at the hospital.

"Oh, Dad. One of these days—these years—you have to come with me, especially if I go to France again. It's so hard to describe." Zoey Bernstein had been promising herself a Paris birthday gift since she was 23 years old. By the time she was 32, she knew she had waited long enough. Her law firm had finally promoted her and given her a substantial bonus, and that bonus funded her trip.

Her father would have been a great traveling partner, but he had demurred. After all, he told her, "You just might meet a handsome Frenchman, and you don't need your father around." She knew that was his excuse *de jour*. He just wasn't ready to travel yet, and Zoey understood why.

"Was the Orsay Museum all you expected it to be? You told me the Claude Monet exhibit is the reason you wanted to spend time there instead of the Louvre."

"Yes, the Orsay had several of Monet's water lily paintings, including *Nymphéas Bleus* and *The Waterlily Pond Green Harmony*. The impressionism exhibit was stunning, Dad. I spent the entire morning reading each of the descriptions in the booklet I bought. It was just so beautiful. I wish you had been there. You know, I did send you plenty of pictures. You did look at them, didn't you!" she frowns as he turns his back to her and stirs the sauce.

"Of course I did." He stops stirring and then points his finger toward the ceiling as if to indicate something he recalls. "I think the picture you sent of you standing with the backdrop of the railway station's clock tower was fabulous. I'm getting that framed."

Zoey decides to let him off the hook about traveling. "Oh, good. Make me a copy, too. Notre Dame was getting closer to opening. I think they set the date for earlier next year. Mostly, there was still fencing all around the cathedral, but I could peek in and see some of the entrance. I heard next Christmas they'll open it up for dignitaries. At least that's what people were saying. It will be spectacular. The Parisians I met were so proud of how well the reconstruction had gone. The biggest highlight for me—the touristy me—was the night cruise on the Seine and seeing the Eiffel Tower glowing with its stunning white lights. It is romance! The City of Light!"

Alan slices open the wrapper on the parmesan cheese and looks up at her. "Ah, romance, huh?"

"Yes, but *no*, Dad. I didn't meet the Parisian love of my life on a one-week vacation in France. And even if I did, I sure wouldn't tell you." She rolls her eyes and then considers, "Now, maybe if I'd stayed longer...."

"Okay, then you need to plan longer vacations."

"I'm not senior enough, Dad, not near senior enough to get away longer than a week. Not yet, anyway." She hops off the stool and sniffs the sauce, then takes the wooden spoon, dips it into the brick-red potion and tastes it. "It tastes just like Mom's." She freezes. After three years, the mention of her mother still stuns the two of them.

A beat. Her father recovers. "I hope my cooking isn't a letdown from the fine cuisine of France."

"Don't be ridiculous, Dad." She scrolls through her phone's pictures and shows him one. "Being a foodie, I took a lot of pics, but this one of my dessert on my last night was just to die for." Again, she cringes at her choice of words. Best to move on, she reasons.

Alan tosses the pasta on the plates and pours the sauce over the top, the meat nestled to the side of each plate. He uses two large spoons to mingle the mixture. Then he grates the parmesan cheese on top. "The wine is the only thing French in this house. I got it for you. You pour, and then we can talk about what's next for you." They sit, smile, and toast to her adventure.

Time drifts by. Talking comes naturally to the two of them. They both know that fathers and daughters do not always have this freedom and ease with each other, but when both father and daughter are lawyers, well, lawyers have a special lexicon. Each knows the other's moves. Once the topic switches from business to their personal lives, however, they are likely to find themselves tongue-tied. The three years that separate them from the lightning strike that took a wife and a mother still cut deeply.

Sophie and Alan's relationship had never failed to make their friends envious. Despite demanding careers, both were dedicated to each other's happiness. Even with decades of marriage behind them, they still held hands on walks and kissed in public.

Sophie had been a hugger, a healer. She had understood the power of human touch. Alan's power was as a visionary. He'd been the planner and the wordsmith.

Now, he has little to plan and less to say.

The next morning, as usual, he reminds himself of the three dimensions in which he feels trapped: He imagines Rod Sterling narrating the beginning of his own personal episode of the *Twilight Zone,* presented in stark black and white.

"Witness Mr. Alan Bernstein. Mr. Bernstein awakens each morning in his small beach cottage near the Pacific Ocean. He sips his freshly brewed coffee and gazes at three framed pictures adorning the sofa table–the photos of his life's triumphs: his picture with his law firm's partners on his retirement; his photo of him and his wife, Sophie, she proudly wearing her pristine white doctor's lab coat for the first time; and his only child Zoey, pictured at her Hastings Law School graduation, beaming with pride between Mr. and Dr. Bernstein."

Sterling strides into the foreground, smoking a cigarette. Alan Bernstein follows along behind him, his athletic 6 feet 4 inches seemingly made smaller and weaker by an obvious, intense loneliness. Sterling glances back at him, then faces the camera lens again and concludes, "This would be an idyllic scene if not for a singular incident that can only be found on the edge ... of the Twilight Zone."

Alan stands and shakes off the last remnants of Rod Sterling. He is so frequently haunted by his past, and last night was a trigger. Being with Zoey inevitably leads to not being with Sophie. How desperately he misses her. How empty each morning feels.

Three years. The pain is supposed to pass. He's been through however many stages of grief that his psychologist has listed. He's talked to friends who say they've felt a similar loss. But it is not the same. It can't be the same. Their loss made some sense. There was some explanation that one could spot in an X-ray or an ending that comes naturally after living life to its fullest.

Zoey's last words to him after dinner had been, "Dad, what's on your agenda tomorrow?"

"I don't know," he'd answered. "I'm retired. I really don't know."

He has things to do, a list he creates each day. A routine.

"Keep busy," they all say.

"Sophie would want you to not just quit on life," they all say.

"You're young. You have so much to offer," they all repeat, and then they go away to find what they're looking for.

*What am I looking for?* Alan Bernstein feels ashamed because he knows he is just wasting time. Time he has been given. Time that was stolen from Sophie.

On his list today is his Tuesday senior league basketball game at the YMCA. Afterwards, he and one of his fellow teammates, his accountant, will have a meeting to discuss his finances. Tom Kent is a good man, always setting Alan up to be in the best position to score in a game ... or at the bank.

## Act 1, Scene 7:
## Sophie

Alan and Tom meet for coffee later that afternoon. The Peet's is empty at 2 pm on a Monday.

"Most people are working, huh?"

"Yeah, "Everybody's 'Working for the Weekend'." Tom pours a dash of milk into his dark brew.

"I've heard that song." Alan eyes his giant peanut butter cookie, splits it carefully into two pieces, and gives the slightly larger portion to Tom. "Weekend? What's a weekend?" They chuckle at the *Downton Abbey* reference.

After some more banter about work and the morning's basketball scrimmage, Tom leans forward to Alan and repeats his familiar mantra, "Alan, you got more money than Rockefeller."

Alan rolls his eyes. He knows his longtime friend thinks he should relax about his finances.

"Seriously, Alan. You should think about a trip somewhere."

"Well, that was the plan. Back then. Sophie and I were planning a trip to London and Scotland, but then ... you know."

"Alan, for God's sake," Tom catches himself, then says softly, "that was three years ago." He whispers, "Come on."

Alan reaches for his coffee and states very deliberately, "Yeah, well, that was what we wanted ... then." The coffee mug descends. "What am I gonna do now? Just travel by myself? I just don't see that happening. Besides, I have things to do."

"Oh, really? Then how come we talk all the time about not having something meaningful to do?"

Alan swirls his coffee around and around. His tell. Tom notices. "I know you, Alan. You are as stubborn as a mule. I'm sure lots of women ... or guys ... you know, would want to travel with you."

"Nobody that I care to travel with other than Zoey. But traveling with her father is, well, it's what it is ... not for a young woman looking for excitement. And me? I don't know, Tom. I just don't...." He sighs.

Alan Bernstein is a man who used to know what he wanted and always went after it. His life had been a series of steps, ascending, always ascending.

And always with Sophie. Despite demanding careers, both had been dedicated to each other's happiness. Even with decades of marriage behind them, they made the effort to keep their romance alive.

Sophie's identity was tied directly to her desire to do what doctors do—reach out even when that stretch is 3,000 miles away. When COVID-19 first hit the Eastern seaboard, her sister, Diana, fell victim. In 2019, doctors were unsure what was happening, so Sophie jumped on the first plane to Providence to help.

Panic was setting in and spreading quickly. Alan was worried. He insisted Sophie take precautions. Whatever those protections were at the time.

Her phone call to him came from the airport. She had landed and was heading to the hospital. "Grabbing a taxi. Love you. Don't worry."

The emergency room was where Dr. Sophie Bernstein had saved lives. Not her own life, though.

Three years ago, Alan and Sophie knew they were ascending. Then the staircase vanished.

Both men sit quietly for a minute.

"I know I have no business telling you what to do with your life," Tom admits. "My two cents is best spent on telling you that money is not your problem. So maybe travel is something that I should shut my trap about."

"No, No. You're right to encourage me. I swear if I found someone that I really enjoyed being with on a trip, I think I'd be ready, but you know, that's not ... I'm just not ready for that kind of relationship. But I always value your opinion."

Alan leans back as Tom leans forward. "What about doing something like volunteering? Didn't you work for the Food Bank? And didn't your firm always put on a holiday dinner at the church? And you used to be on some committees...."

Allan corrects him, "No. Sophie was on lots of committees. She pushed me to do things. The Food Bank was good. I did it for years, but then, I dunno. It just became something I didn't look forward to. I was doing it out of guilt."

"Wait. Sophie, wasn't she the president of the community theater, what's it called?"

"Oh, the ... the, geeze, I can't remember shit anymore. Wait. The La Paloma Playhouse. How can I forget that? We never missed a show. Yeah, she was the president for a term, and she was always involved."

Tom nods, "And I imagine she ... Sophie ... she'd love that you got involved there somehow, don't you think?"

Alan nods. "Well, sure. God, is it still open? I thought it closed up during COVID."

"No. I don't think so. Callie was just telling me about a play she wanted to see there. At least, I think it was there. Maybe. Anyway, if it is, you might wanna look into it. Maybe they need a booster. Like you, Mr. Moneybags."

"I could look into it. Let me think about it. That's something Sophie would really want me to ... to care about."

## Act 1, Scene 8:
## Little Italy

"Molly, we are on a mission!"

"And our first road trip in a long, long time," Molly replies.

Callie's Subaru is carrying baggage, some full, some empty. First stop: Little Italy, twenty miles south of Encinitas. They are meeting Carlo and Carmen at their one-bedroom condo.

During their dinner at Carmen's, it was Carlo who pulled up a chair when they were discussing Molly's move from Los Angeles. He apologized at the time, saying, "I am sorry but I hear much when I go back and forth from table to table, and when I hear you are moving here ... well, like my wife and I ... we, too, came here and ... I hope Molly can understand that we have been friends with Tom and Callie for so long, and they did much for us back then and ... well, let me just tell you about where we first came here, okay? Just hear, okay? No have to decide anything, okay? Good."

Callie accelerates onto the 5 freeway heading south as Molly reflects on her good fortune, "I can't believe that they offered their condo to me until the end of the year." Molly peers out the passenger window to scan the beachfront of Del Mar. It's another blue sky, onshore breeze August day. She can see the stands of the Del Mar Race Track, which has occupied this pristine landscape for as long as she can remember. It was all the rage in the heyday of Bing Crosby and the Hollywood stars of yesteryear.

The California State Fair was just hosted at the track with musical guests entertaining nightly crowds. Now, thoroughbreds are racing there, and locals will once again remind tourists that this is "where the surf meets the turf in Ol' Del Mar." Naturally, proprietors of all the local businesses will charge hefty prices to these tourists. Locals, of course, know how to trot right around the inflated prices.

Within minutes, Molly sees the scene shift to the cliffs of Torrey Pines, and just as quickly to the two "beach party" towns for the younger set: first, Pacific Beach and then Ocean Beach.

"You remember when we used to go dancing in PB, Callie?"

"Yep. At Don Diego's. The guys were cute and the beers were cheap."

"If I recall, it was margaritas that were your vice."

"Yeah, well, that was when we were—I was—pretty foolish." Callie veers right on the 5 freeway as they pass Old Town's Mexican cafes, the setting for Bruce Springsteen's song "Rosalita."

Molly smiles at the vision of those bygone days. She rolls down the window to let the breeze blow her hair back. "Okay, you were a bigger partier than I was, granted. But I was the better dancer."

Callie counters, "And a flirt, too. I had to get you out of a few bars back then when the guys were ready to toss you onto their shoulders and abscond with you."

"I know. You never let me forget that. I have thanked you a million times for saving me. Remember that one guy ... what was his name? Oh, wait, I remember. Chad. He thought he was John Travolta out there." They both start laughing and, within a minute, Callie starts snorting. Molly yells, "Stop it. Stop. We're gonna crash."

Callie is trying to see through her snorts. She manages to exit the freeway in the Port District. At the stoplight, she blurts out, "Remember how he was thrusting his hips out like in the old movie!"

"Yes. Yes. But then he went into some bizarre version of the Electric Slide and tried to get ... get (she is gasping for breath) ... get everyone to do it (more snorting) even though the song was not the "Electric Boogie'!" Another wave of laughter crashes into the front seat, only to stop abruptly when the car behind them blares its horn.

Both sisters jump, and Callie hits the gas. She manages to avoid the car in front of them and yells at her sister, "Stop talking. Please. And start looking for a parking place!"

They are now in Little Italy, where 6,000 Italian fishermen in the 1920s created the legendary four blocks that make up the village. After a turn or two, they spot a parking place on Columbia Street. They look in the mirrors to check their faces, touch up smudged mascara, and slide out of the car doors. They try not to look at each other out of fear that they will lose all sense of adulthood.

Molly starts walking to the cafe where Carlo and Carmen will be meeting them. Callie is a step behind, making sure she's locked the car and will remember where in the world they parked. Carlo and Carmen are waving to them at the historic Amici House. The twins wave back.

Carlo and Carmen kiss each of the women on both cheeks, and then Carlo presents himself as tour guide and historian. "This house is, no was, no is, ah! Pardon my English. Past. Present. So confusing. Anyway, this was the home in 1916 owned by Mr. Antonino Giacalone and his wife. He was a fisherman just like his neighbors back then. *Capiche?* Yes. see. We go down this street to India Street. I don't know why *India* is the name. It should be *Italy Street.* Yes. Come. Come."

When they get to their condo, Carmen explains, "This is where we moved once we got to America. Carlo and I, we had family here, and they let us stay until we find a small place. See if you like."

The women learn that here is where Carmen and Carlo's American adventure began. They sold their restaurant in Milan, but before that, they applied for citizenship in the United States. "It took two year," Carmen tells the ladies. "I pray it not take so long. Ah, like you say, 'It is what it is.' We work here in many places to get more money and know what's what before we finally buy our bistro, where we met you, Molly."

Meanwhile, Carlo is giving a tour of the condo. He is a ball of energy, pointing and spinning from corner to corner.

"It is adorable, Carlo. I can't accept that you will not let me pay you. I must pay for the utilities at least. I insist." Molly asserts.

"Okay. Okay. But that is all. This is where my ... our family stay when they visit. But nobody coming the rest of the year. So it is yours. Is *perfetto.* And you being a famous actress!"

Carmen interjects, "Watch out for the men here, Molly! Italians, crazy for you. Even the old ones can be a pain. They touch. They whistle. They don't know it not nice. *Attendo!*" All four chuckle at her warning.

"So you have a home near Callie and Tom, right?" Molly asks.

"Yes. It's very nice. Much bigger for the boys, too. We open the restaurant in 2018, and all was going so good. People loved Carmen's cooking. We make many, many friends. Like Callie and Tom. I don't think we met you then, did we?" Carlo points to his head as if there is a memory button he can push to boot up a face.

"No. I was doing ... acting projects."

"Ah. Of course. Then. BOOM! The COVID hits us and we are so worried we lose everything. But people were so nice. Americans, very generous. They kept us open with takeaway food ... you say 'takeout' right? Right. And they give us big tips. Big tips. So the family made it. Carmen, she was a nervous wreck."

Carmen, who is biting her nails at the memory, nods. "When Carlo hear you talk at dinner about moving and where to stay, we say 'We know where, right here!'"

"Yes. During big pandemic is when Tom and Callie were so nice to us. So this is our chance to ... how you say ... give back to *Bella Donna,* Molly." Carlo is so pleased with himself, he can't stand still. "You like our Little Italy?"

"Oh, I like! I *love* it."

"Is no Hollywood with movie stars," Carmen has stopped biting her nails.

"No, thank God it is not."

They walk to the nearest cafe for an espresso, and as they cross the street, Molly can see that Little Italy is just a block from the harbor. There is a park between the water and the train tracks that run through the village. She sees people playing bocce ball in the distance.

She knows that if she walks south and turns into the city, she will be in the heart of downtown. The cafe they stroll into is in the piazza on India Street, where vendors are also selling fresh fruit and vegetables.

Molly takes in the scene at the cafe. Four old men, each sipping their coffees in demitasse cups, are loudly boasting to each other in Italian. It reminds her of a Scorsese movie with Deniro, Pacino, Sorvino, and Brando all puffing out their chests.

They order coffee. Carlo insists on treating.

Eventually, Callie explains they have to get going to beat the Los Angeles traffic, if one can ever beat the clogged arteries of L.A.

As Molly and Callie leave their hosts, they pass several clothing boutiques and bistros and newer upscale restaurants. There is a quaintness, a European flavor, that is settled over this village. The neighborhood is a far cry from Hollywood, where the motto is "Celebrity, Heal Thyself."

Little Italy is just what the doctor ordered.

## Act 1, Scene 9:
# Say Goodbye to Hollywood

Thirty years of memories. Molly has never been a hoarder, but she has accumulated a lot of memorabilia. Awards. Posters. Programs. Ticket stubs. And photos with so many of her mentors. What to let go of? What to keep? What to cherish?

What to take with her? What would even fit in storage? What to give away? What to sell? What's worth anything to anyone but her?

With Callie's help, it takes a week and a half to sort through it all. This should give her time to shake off the trepidation that is inevitable when making such a significant transition. However, bundling retirement, separating from her acting family, relying on and reuniting with her twin sister and brother-in-law, and watching the HOLLYWOOD sign fade in the distance from her rearview mirror naturally raises her level of anxiety.

And on top of that, here's Leo.

"So, it looks like you *are* serious." Leo is taking in the barren living room. His face reflects his surprise that Molly is actually deserting him, that she is no longer bluffing or acting out of frustration. "I see you're selling, not leasing or renting. Hmm. I guess it's my challenge to get you back on the horse."

"Oh, Leo. That horse bucked me off years ago. You are not my agent anymore. You *are* my forever friend, but there's no going back now." Molly extends her hands and grasps his, now bony and aged, worn from handshakes consummating optimistic deals and dried out from deals that went south.

"Well, look. You aren't moving across the country—like back in the New York days or those crazy touring years." He squeezes her hands, foreshadowing his next pitch. "I've got connections in San Diego, you know. It's becoming a theater town with the Old Globe and ..."

"Leo. Stop. That's ridiculous. I am so removed from that scene, and that scene is so removed from me. You just don't want to admit that I am past my prime. If I ever truly had a *prime.*"

Callie busies herself in the kitchen packing the last of the dishes and glasses. The breakable things. She hopes that her sister does not break under Leo's persistent attempts to lure her back into showbiz.

"Here me out, Molly. I know they are auditioning at two of the local rep theaters, and I got word they're shooting some nice commercials for the snowbirds' winter tourism. I can connect you to my people."

Molly's hands have abandoned Leo's and found a home in her hair.

"Leo, I do NOT want to be rude or unappreciative! But you need to understand that I am starting a new life. I'm focused on moving forward. Living in a new city. Helping Callie take care of my father, who we're losing every day." She takes a breath.

"I have no energy for or interest in rewinding the tape of my *career.* I have other plans. I don't know what, yet. But I am done morphing myself into a fictional character. I am *Molly O'Toole.* You are Leo Grabarkowitz. You are an agent to the stars. I am no longer a star, if I ever was." Molly's arms extend out so that her body becomes a cross.

Leo looks at her and scowls. But then, his old never-say-die expression rearranges itself like a Rubik's cube rotating and stops at something akin to the look a fisherman has when he's sure the hook remains in his catch. He just needs to let the fish run, tire itself out, and reel her in. *Patience. Someday she will come back. It's in her blood.* But seeing her so defiant brings his emotions to the surface. He has only one recourse.

He stands.

Molly stands.

Callie wipes her hands on a dishtowel and enters downstage, facing them.

Suddenly, it hits all three, as if the movie suddenly goes dark and the credits of one's life roll up the screen. And with that finality, Molly's tears come, and this scene fades to black.

## Act 1, Scene 10:
# An Actress's Nightmare

It takes two weeks to evacuate an anxious Molly from her 30-year engagement with the City of Angels. Each evening after a day spent sorting, packing, discarding and cleaning, she and Callie stroll along Hollywood's Avenue of the Stars with its Walk of Fame. There are more than two thousand five-pointed stars embedded in the sidewalks commemorating Hollywood greats. Under their feet, they see Sophia Loren, retired but still the Star of Italy. And Gregory Peck, the handsome classic Hollywood star, who exists now only in film and memories. And Gene Kelly, too, one of the finest to dance across the silver screen.

"They don't make 'em like they used to," Callie whispers to Molly.

"No. They don't. But in those days, the studio owned them, and they were happy to be purchased. They thought they were the lucky ones. And I suppose they were. Generations of us after that hoped that our names would be up there." She glances at the Pantages Theater's marquee. "Or down here." She laughs, stepping aside to avoid walking on Debbie Reynolds.

"Well, you had ... um, have been in the spotlight, though."

"Sure," Molly concedes. "It's addictive. The attention. The excitement! I'll never forget when I was in that movie with Paul Newman. I think it was his last one."

"Which movie?" Callie looks down, hoping to see Newman's star beneath her feet.

"*Road to Perdition.* Sure, Tom Hanks is a great guy and cute, but when I was standing right next to Paul, I almost fainted. He leaned into me and said something about how nice I looked in costume. Jesus, he was a freaking dream!"

"His blue eyes!"

Molly shakes her head, "His everything. Can you imagine, Callie, being around him in the 70's in *The Sting* or *Butch Cassidy* with Redford? They were so cool."

"That's Old Hollywood, huh?"

"Yeah. In my early days, the movies in the 90s for someone like me trying to break in, well, those films were kinda lame. *Clueless. Cruel Intentions....*"

Callie tosses out her gum. "The titles said it all, huh?"

"But when I got in a scene with Bill Murray in ..."

"Groundhog Day."

"Right! God, you remember everything about my films."

Callie stops walking and pivots to face her sister. "Duh. I've watched *Groundhog Day* at least ten times. Every time, I stop it at your scene when you're standing with the people looking to see if the stupid groundhog sees his shadow."

"Yeah. Murray was so damn funny. It was impossible to keep a straight face. He broke us up every time the director wanted to reshoot the scenes. He would say it was *literally* Groundhog Day."

They both laugh. Then Callie snorts, and they have to stop and compose themselves. After a minute, she grabs Molly's hand, and the two of them keep up their slow pace. "I remember when you were the *star witness* on *Law and Order.*

And I loved you as one of the secretaries who was always fighting off the lecherous men in that show ... um ..."

"*Mad Men.* Yeah, but that was also real life, honey. It didn't do wonders for my marriage. Although by then Kurt was already cheating on me multiple times."

"He started it, though."

"Yeah, he did, and when he promised it was never gonna happen again, I was the sucker."

Callie reminds her, "Turnabout is fair play."

"Not really."

"I didn't mean that your affair was right ... or fair." Callie is attempting to apologize.

"No. I know what you mean. I was just so pissed off at him. I was lonely. Angry. All of it at once."

Molly pauses a moment to watch as two couples hurry along the sidewalk toward the Pantages Theatre. Being late for the show matters to these couples. But not for Molly. Molly's Walk of Fame is over.

So is their evening walk. They've arrived back at Callie's car. They hop in. Callie pulls out and then recalls a wonderful memory. "Remember when I flew out to see you in *Hairspray?* God! That was so awesome. You took me backstage and introduced me to the dancers and even the lead actress. What was her name?"

"Marissa Jaret Winokur played Tracy Turnblad," Molly replies. "I was having the best time that night." Her voice drops half an octave. "For half the day. Then I got homesick and lonely. All I could think about was getting back to the theater and starting the show all over. Then one night, Meryl Streep came backstage after the show, and I couldn't even speak when she introduced herself to me ... to the cast ... like she needed to ... like we didn't already know who she was. I can tell you that there is such a thing as *starstruck.*" She shakes her head, trying to dissolve this scene from the past and return to the present.

Molly glances back at the Pantages sign fading into the distance. "I was a roadie then, in a way. Going from audition to audition. Sometimes in one show and then another. All bit parts until ... there was no more."

They stop at a red light.

"Yeah, just like this. A red light. I just stopped while everyone else kept going right in front of my eyes."

Quiet. Nothing is said the rest of the way.

Back home, Molly tries to let the past fade away as she lays her head on the pillow. Within seconds, as is her pattern, she is lost in a semi-conscious world that is part fantasy, part reality. A swirl of the nonsensical.

Her dreams make sense as bizarre vignettes. Like someone took four jigsaw puzzles and broke up the pieces, then tossed them together in a mishmash of non-sequiturs.

She is part of a gaggle of reporters shouting questions at CJ Craig in the press room of *The West Wing*... Monica from *Friends* sits next to her and orders a latte ... Molly rises to get her the coffee but is suddenly in complete darkness ... An actor playing George opposite her when she played Nancy in the play *An Actor's Nightmare* looks at her and asks "What play am I in now?" ... She is holding a clipboard that belongs to her character because she is the stage manager in the play ... She tells George, "You are Prince Hamlet, for Christ's sake! Don't you know your lines?" ... "No!" he yells at her. "I am not Hamlet! I'm not even an actor. Who are you? ...

*A light shines suddenly in her eyes, and a man with a baseball hat yells at her,* "NEVER. NEVER. NEVER LOOK DIRECTLY INTO THE CAMERA, YOU IDIOT! YOU ARE A GODDAMN EXTRA IN THIS FREAKING COMMERCIAL!"

Molly erupts from her bed. Her night sweats have soaked her nightgown. She is wide awake and scared to death.

She wills herself out of bed and searches in the darkness for her robe. She refuses to wake her sister. They need to be on the road tomorrow to get to her new digs. She grits her teeth and murmurs to herself, *Say Goodbye to Hollywood*, then quietly slips into the bathroom, changes her nightgown, and sits on the tiled floor in the dark, leaning against the bathtub.

Callie finds her in the morning, sound asleep on the cold tiles.

"Oh, poor thing."

# Act 2:
# The Arrival

## Act 2, Scene 1:
# The La Paloma Playhouse

A week after Tom's conversation with Alan about volunteering at the La Paloma Playhouse, Alan's second act began with a call to Renee and Patrick Swanson, the owners.

The call could not have come at a better time. Sophie's death, followed by COVID, had devastated the theater, and the Swansons were looking for something, anything, that would help it survive.

The La Paloma had been built in the late 1920s, the only movie house on northern San Diego's picturesque coastline. The first film shown was "The Cohens and Kellys in Paris." It was a gala event reported in the 1991 Encinitas Magazine as having been attended by Hollywood starlet and soon-to-be Academy Award winner Mary Pickford. It has been rumored that "she rode her bicycle eleven miles to the La Paloma from Fairbanks Ranch for the event."

Back then, the La Paloma had theater seats direct from New York, velvet curtains, a state-of-the-art pipe organ for the silent films, and pictures of chaste maidens on the ceiling. Eight decades later, however, most of the seats were filthy or broken, the velvet curtains were ripped and on the floor, and the maidens had faded to pale pink and blue.

Renee and Patrick bought the theater dirt cheap, but then had to remodel it, install all the necessary lighting, and construct a stage that would accommodate a live theater production. A year after the work and the expense, patrons were beginning to realize that a performance at the La Paloma was not something to miss, and the new owners were seeing some meager dividends. Ten years after that, they had a sizable subscriber audience, had expanded the seating, and were hosting more elaborate productions.

The Swansons' history with La Paloma was almost as interesting as Mary Pickford's rumored history had once been. When Renee and Patrick met in 1998, each had their own small business. Renee owned a salon and Patrick a guitar store that doubled as a place for music lessons.

Patrick had the backing of his well-to-do family, which encouraged his interest in music. He was an undisciplined sixteen-year-old punk rocker in a band called the Slashers. That was the first of a half-dozen startup, flameout local bands where his guitar riffs were the only thing ever mentioned by a critic. Failure speaks louder than riffs, however, so he shifted to vocals, with no particular success at that, either. Then, he left the punk scene to try to break into musical theater. The spirit was willing, but his vocals ... not so much.

Eventually, he gained enough maturity to realize he needed to give up the spotlight and focus on tutoring and sales, and this got him a partnership with the Moonlight Music Shoppe. It took five years and a loan from his parents, but Patrick became the owner of the shop and a favorite of locals who had the same ambitions he had once had.

Further down Encinitas's Highway 101 was the Flawless Touch Salon. Renee Aveline, whose family had immigrated from France when she was only ten years old, had become the sole proprietor after buying out her two other partners.

Being a beauty shop owner had not been the dream of Renee's parents for their daughter. They'd invested in her college education, but Renee had dropped out after one semester. Her dream then had been to dress like Cyndi Lauper—and then magically morph into a model, actress and pop singer all rolled into one.

As it was with Patrick, the dream died. After ten years of trying on trendy clothes that she couldn't afford to buy, rushing to auditions but never getting the part, and singing in the shower because no record label had any interest in a naive, young girl with big dreams and little formal training, she had settled into cosmetology.

To her credit, she'd thrown herself headlong into beauty and style. She'd partnered with two other like-minded women, purchased a rundown barbershop, and built up a solid clientele. The business thrived due to her shrewd business sense, partly acquired from her mother, a successful accountant. Her two partners then married and had children, and they both took her up on offers to buy them out and become the sole proprietor. For her, it was a *Flawless Touch*.

It was inevitable that Renee and Patrick, two indie souls, would meet at various music and art festivals downtown. They embraced each other's artistic passions. After months of amorous advances, they decided to marry. With their love for the arts and their mutual ambitions, it was as inevitable that when the La Paloma came up for sale, Patrick would sell his music shop and the two would purchase the playhouse and pursue a shared passion.

One night, as a favor to a rich benefactor, the Rolling Stones played a set at the La Paloma and made the theater a celebrated venue. After that, the Swansons were able to book not only stage plays but also famous celebrities from the world of comedy, music and dance.

Their dream became more of a reality when Sophie Bernstein stepped in to become their board president. She became the liaison to artists in the community, famous hometown surfers, a prominent local rock band, and former students from Patrick's high school.

Sophie had been a La Paloma institution. With Alan by her side, she had served in every capacity, from president to ticket sales manager. She'd even occasionally made a cameo acting appearance. It had all seemed like a storybook ending—until the COVID pandemic and her tragic death.

The La Paloma Playhouse went dark for the better part of two years. Even after it opened again, many of its patrons feared catching COVID. So they didn't attend performances. Patrick and Renee didn't have much in emergency funds and had to apply for business loans. Some wealthier citizens and several loyal businesses also helped out. But it wasn't enough. The couple had been unwilling to speak with Alan concerning their woes. They knew that Sophie's death had consumed him, and they didn't feel it was right to burden him further.

So, when Alan called and told them he felt he had to continue Sophie's commitment to the theater, they were overjoyed and quite relieved.

## Act 2 Scene 2:
# Renee and Patrick

Alan has arranged to meet the Sorensons at the La Paloma Playhouse on Monday morning. He knows that the theater is dark today, and he has brought coffee for the couple, as he promised on the phone. When Sophie was the president of the theater, she often would meet with Renee and Patrick for coffee on days the theater was closed. Alan has decided to keep that tradition alive.

As he opens the door to the lobby, he notices the details, as is his penchant. It has been at least two years since he's been here. The lobby seems to be unchanged, and that fact perturbs him. He recalls it looking smart; it now looks tired. Posters are from plays produced long ago, and the drapes droop. He peers into the auditorium, where he can see that some of the chairs are worn and the taupe carpet has taken on a gray-brown tinge.

"Hello," he calls out. "Is there anyone here?"

Renee appears from behind the red curtain, "Alan! Alan, we are thrilled you called. We're so happy to see you."

She moves to give him a hug. He places his coffee tray with the three coffees on a table near the auditorium entrance, first checking to make sure it's sturdy, and only then smiles broadly and embraces Renee. *Security first, always.*

"We missed you so much." Renee is on tiptoes, the top of her head barely reaching Alan's chin. Their embrace lifts her off her feet.

"Renee, oh, Renee. I've been so foolish. I should have never allowed so much time to go by. It's been far too long." Alan lowers Renee, brushes his gray hair back, and removes his sunglasses. "You look terrific. Where's Patrick?"

On cue, Patrick's voice echoes from somewhere in the theater's bowels. "I'm on my way, Alan. I'm just adjusting a light."

"I have coffee here and a little pastry to go with it," Alan bellows into the darkness as Renee pulls out a chair for him at the table. "I'm sorry. I tried to time it better, but I am a little early."

Renee takes a coffee off the tray and sips it. "Don't be ridiculous, Alan. We're just running around like chickens with our heads cut off. It's been one of those crazy weeks. Actually, it's been a crazy run with this latest play, but it's closing this Sunday." She looks up at him. "Alan, I'd forgotten how tall you are. You are always so debonair, so they say."

"As who says?"

"Oh, don't be so modest, Mister. You always had the looks of a movie star. It's a shame we could never get you to step onto our stage. We would have had an audience filled with ladies!"

"Oh, no, you wouldn't have. You would have had an empty house, at least after I froze up and forgot my lines. I couldn't even read parts with Sophie when she was practicing her parts. Even thinking about being on stage made me a wreck."

Thinking he has now moved the conversation away from any further embarrassing compliments or talk about him becoming an actor, Alan puts a touch of sugar in his coffee. "I asked them to give me cream, too. I know Patrick takes his coffee with cream."

Patrick arrives, and he and Alan give each other a brotherly hug. "Oh, my God, Alan, it's so good to see you.

Renee told me we were meeting you here, and I said, 'Why? Why not have him over for dinner?'"

Renee cuts in. "Patrick always thinks we should have people 'over for dinner,' like that's why they call." Patrick nods, implying she's right. As usual.

Alan remembers those dinners. They were always a foursome, brought together by Sophie, who would invite Patrick and Renee to their house to discuss the theater. They would be invited to one of Swanson's dinners on their birthdays.

Alan isn't quite ready to cross that bridge yet.

The threesome chat about nothing and everything, small talk that Alan realizes is intended to make him feel at ease. He leans toward them, and they toward him, as though the time they have lost since last seeing each other can be minimized now by physical closeness.

Alan updates them on his daughter. "Zoey has done wonderful work for her law firm." He pauses, then makes up his mind to speak the unspoken. "I wish with all my heart that her mother could see her. She would be cheering from the courtroom gallery—if a judge let her—at how passionate and polished Zoey is. Sophie always knew that Zoey was born to be a lawyer. She knew it from the moment Zoey started school."

Silence. They nod. Each picks up their cup of coffee and takes a sip. Then, slowly, they place the paper cups down to silently signify that one bridge has been crossed.

Patrick approaches a second bridge: "Well, Alan, we haven't asked you how *you're* doing. Everyone we know is wondering how *Alan Bernstein* is handling retirement. It's been how long since you retired?" He leans back now to take in Alan's report.

"Yes, Alan, what are you doing with yourself these days? You were, let's admit it, a bit of a workaholic." Renee reaches out and puts her hand on Alan's. "What's on your *docket*... isn't that how attorneys word it?"

Alan straightens up and fixes his open collar so it sits just right, with equal space between the buttons of his collar. "Well, that's part of why I wanted to speak with you both. I'll be honest. Retirement is definitely an adjustment. Change is not easy for me. I was accustomed to go, go, go. When I finally stopped racing from crisis to client to court, well, it was like jumping off a merry-go-round and finding your balance is completely distorted. So, I guess, you could say I am a work in progress, getting my retirement legs under me."

"Totally understandable, Alan," Renee smiles. "We are all walking a tightrope trying to balance our ambitions with our limitations. I'm afraid COVID did a number on us here at the theater ... and throughout the world, so no pity party for us."

Alan responds, "So the pandemic did 'a number' on you guys. I assume being closed for, what, a year I guess, it had to be a financial hit. But when I talk to people or read the local paper, you seem to have rebounded. Am I being naive?"

Patrick sighs. "We put on a good face. It's part of the acting biz. But the truth is we are just barely getting by. People are not coming back to a public theater. I mean, some are afraid, some are still sick, and sadly, some have passed from COVID or just lost the will to live. It was a terrible thing. Community is so important. Loneliness is a killer in itself. Generally, community theaters like ours count on the support of seniors, and that support is waning."

"Oh. I had no idea." Alan stops himself and realizes he is not being straight with them or himself. Missing Sophie, COVID, and his retirement anxiety surge like a wave and crash into him. Renee and Patrick wait for him to speak his truth.

"Actually, that is a copout. I lost Sophie. Then I lost myself. Just like everyone, I accepted being lonely as the new normal, and I closed my eyes and kept busy round the clock. I don't think I realized just how empty my life is until I stopped working. Thank goodness for Zoey. But I get it. You two have been heroes in this community, and this theater has to thrive. That's why I called and why I wanted to meet you both." Alan comes up for air.

He leans back as the wave recedes and takes a moment before the next wave brings them together.

"First, I want to make a donation to the theater. I've been told by Tom Kent, my accountant, that I'm in good shape—actually, he called me 'Mr. Moneybags.' He knows how to needle me. But far more important to me personally is I want to have some skin in the game. I want to volunteer to work here, you know, do whatever. I'm pretty handy with power tools, and I'm sure you could use a tall guy to do some of the heavy lifting."

Smiles all around. "Oh, yeah, we sure could use you, Alan. As a matter of fact, what are you doing this coming Sunday?"

Renee puts her hand up. "Patrick, you don't have to jump on him like that. He just practically sat down here."

"I know, but ..."

"No, no, Renee, I'm retired. I have more time on my hands than I know what to do with. Sunday is a great day for me. What's up?"

"We're closing the show and striking the set. It's a tradition. And then we get pizza for everyone. The cast and crew. You'll get to meet lots of folks. Some you already know and others ... newbies, who have joined our merry band." Patrick is pleased with himself and looks at Renee, who nods in agreement.

"Well, say no more. Just tell me when and I'll have my toolbelt at the ready." They break into laughter.

Later, as he leaves the theater, Alan looks back at the sign of the La Paloma Playhouse. Two doves have landed on top of it. The symbolism does not escape him. Sophie would be reminding him that *La Paloma* in Spanish means *the dove*.

The doves are nesting. As is he.

## Act 2, Scene 3:
# Molly Tours the Town

Molly O'Toole's second act begins in her new neighborhood in Little Italy. Her cozy condo, which she is "housesitting"—that's how Carlo put it—is on Columbia Street. Since her first day here, she has been out and about, but she wants to get the lay of the land by booking a walking tour.

"Are you sure a walking tour isn't some touristy, old-person thing?" Callie asks her when the two are talking on the phone.

Molly is tart. "First, I *am* a tourist. Second, I am definitely old. But more important, this tour includes wine tasting and food nibbling at various *piazzas*, so it is a perfect fit for me." Molly has read about the history of this part of San Diego, and she wants to know where a single, kinda lonely, retired woman can hang out. "Callie, it's time for me to bust outta Hollywood and my past!"

"Okay, good idea, Molly. Just don't get too liquored up and then get busted."

"Ha, ha. Very funny."

The tour guide, Gia, is tall and middle-aged. She begins with the history of the four or so blocks that make up Little Italy. "We are at the Waterfront Bar and Grill. It's a popular hangout for the young and restless." She laughs. So does Molly and the dozen of her new companions. "But you will notice that it is crowded with many not-so-young folks. That is because it's daytime. Now, does anyone know why it is called the *Waterfront?*"

She pauses for an answer. As usual, no one wants to be foolish. But one woman wearing a tacky pink sweatshirt with bold letters proclaiming she is an "*L.A.* Doll" offers the obvious, "Because the water is here?"

Gia replies diplomatically. "Well, the water is a mile away, but you are on the right track. This is where the ocean flowed into the bay, but that was decades ago when this was a fisherman's wharf. The city elders decided that this entire area behind us would be a landfill, and everything you see to the west exists so there would be more ground to build businesses and Waterfront Park, which is a popular walking path for all the locals. Thus, this Waterfront Bar marks the spot where Little Italy and its Italian fishermen wet their whistles. So to speak."

Molly takes note of both the bar scene and the walking path. She smiles at the thought of a sunset stroll so different from her previous, far less picturesque, Sunset Boulevard walks.

Gia takes the group up the numbered streets and eventually to the historic highlights: "Our Lady of the Rosary Catholic Church built in 1925, which has guided our fishermen to the shore," to the six *piazzas: Basilone, Pescatore, Giannini, Villiaggio, Constanza*, and the most famous and largest, *Piazza della Famiglia.* Then *to* "The Amici House, built in 1916."

Molly tunes out Gia momentarily because Carlo and Carmen have already given her the background on this landmark. She steps into the shade to cool off and watch the people on India Street, in the heart of the village. They are of all ages, clearly a mix of tourists and the people who live in the apartments and condos above some of the buildings. As it is a warm, late summer day, shorts and crop tops are the fashion for the ladies. Sunglasses are ubiquitous and seem to be such that almost every woman's entire face is hidden. Perhaps, she thinks, that is how they want to be. Mysterious.

Amici Park gets her attention. Most people would be attracted to its quaint umbrella-covered tables and chairs, good for reading, but what really strikes her is the bocce ball park and the men and women gathered around the tubular playing field. They are laughing loudly, as many Italians are wont to do. "Gia, I see people playing bocce ball. Is that something open to the public?" she asks.

"Oh, yes! You could just go down there and watch and then ask to play." Gia tilts her head to Molly. "I'm quite sure those older gentlemen I see there would love to have you join their game. I'm not so sure the women with them would be as eager."

Molly and Gia smile at each other.

Eventually, the group stops for wine tasting at the *Piazza della Famiglia.* Gia explains its significance to the Italian immigrants who found San Diego's bayfront home: "Piazza della Famiglia is dedicated to the past, present, and future families of the Little Italy neighborhood. It has become a central community gathering place, hosting farmers' markets, concerts, cultural events, and much more. It is a little slice of what an Italian village would be. As you can see, the ocean view makes it a perfect place for our wine tasting and, of course, dinners. We have wonderful trattorias along India Street and just off the main avenue."

After the hour-long tour and the wine tastings from three different restaurants, Gia cheers as pizza slices are delivered by a strikingly handsome, young waiter. "*Prego. Prego. Angelo!* My people, this is from Isola Pizza Bar, which is just down the street. *Prego, Angelo."*

Molly takes a bite of the classic cheese pizza and is reminded of great pizzas in New York.

Other members of the group finish their pizza, thank Gia for making the afternoon fun, and slip away. Before the guide can also make her exit, Molly approaches her. "Gia, can I ask you for a recommendation for a yoga studio and a salon? I just moved here and am trying to figure out what would be a good fit for me."

"Gosh, there are too many yoga studios to name, and I am not sure what you'd prefer. But all of them will give you a free class or even a week to decide. They are very accommodating because there's so much competition."

"Nice to know."

"As for a salon, The Flawless Touch is my favorite, hands down. The catch is it is in Encinitas."

"Oh, that's no problem. My sister lives there and I have a car. The Flawless Touch, okay. I'll put that in my contacts."

"Yes, yes. The owner, Renee, is wonderful. I've known her for years. You have to tell her I sent you. I'm sure she'll take special care of you. Wait ... you just moved here?"

"Yes. So I am a little bit like a tourist." They both laugh.

"Where did you move from?"

Molly hesitates. "Oh, you don't want to know ... or if I tell you, you'll probably groan."

"No. I won't."

"Okay. L.A."

"No."

"Yes. See, I've learned one thing about San Diegans. They do not like LA. But really, I moved from Hollywood."

"Hollywood! Oh, that's much better. Are you an actress?" Gia, who herself is spry and full of energy, steps back to get a full-length view of the petite woman before her. "Of course, you have the beauty, and just the way you carry yourself ... a dancer, too, perhaps?"

Molly is slightly embarrassed, but she counters, "Gia, you are too kind, but I am far too short to be a dancer. I *was* an actress. I've retired and left that crazy world."

"Okay, I won't ask you for any Hollywood gossip." Gia leans in to hug Molly and says, "I'm sure my Little Italy will suit you well. But watch out for the Italian men here. They are so forward. You know what I mean?" It's a warning but delivered with a smile.

Molly nods. "I got the same warning from my sister. Message received." They embrace again, and this time Gia kisses Molly on both cheeks.

"It is a custom here," Gia says. "Remember, Renee at The Flawless Touch." She waves goodbye.

"*Prego*! Gia. I will."

Molly heads back to her condo to get off her feet. She has definitely gotten the lay of the land.

# Act 2, Scene 4:
# Liam's Par for the Course

"Daddy, are you sure you're up for this?" Callie's speaking to her father, but she's looking at his nurse, Laurie. Molly frowns. Her father seems more frail in just the last few months. Each visit makes Molly wonder just how much longer her father can remain even a shadow of the man she's known. Both his mind and body are failing him.

Even though her father is telling her he feels fine, Callie waits for the nurse to respond. "I think Mr. O'Toole needs to be careful. You both need to guide him. I know you've taken him out to the putting green before, but lately he's struggling to stay balanced." Laurie hesitates, then relents. "I tell you what. I will send an aide out with you. Remember, your father weakens quickly."

Molly takes a breath. Maybe taking her father for a walk outside to the patch of carpeting that poses as a two-hole putting green is too iffy. "Callie, are you sure we should push it?"

"He will love it, Molly. Every time I've done this with him before, he rallies. It keeps his spirits up. Don't worry. We will be right there with him."

Molly decides that Callie's experience with her father trumps her lack of time with him. "Okay."

With the aide following behind them, Liam, balanced by his walker, shuffles out the door of the memory care wing to the lobby, and then out the side door to the landscaped garden and benches. He doesn't want to sit down and rest there, but the sisters insist. "Oh, all right. Christ almighty. You two are gonna make me late for my tee time. I wonder if the guys are waiting for me." Liam looks around, straining his neck to see his imaginary foursome.

Molly looks to Callie, who shrugs and then whispers, "Remember, I told you he usually thinks he's on a golf course with his old pals. He'll start talking to them. Listen."

"Okay. I'm ready. Let's get to the first tee." Liam is up and heading toward the putting green. When he gets there, he sets his walker aside, reaches for his putter in Callie's hand, and leans on that. "Great to have a caddie, huh, Harry?"

He reaches into the pocket of his sagging pants and produces his favorite white golf ball. He drops it at his feet. "Seems to me this is gonna break left to right, don't ya think, Charlie?"

He then leans on the putter for balance and swings the club far too hard, sending the ball bouncing off the cement bumper and stopping at the far end of the carpeting.

"Um, Dad, you don't know your own strength!" This is from Callie.

"What? What did you say, Harry?" Liam looks up at the aide sitting on the bench opposite them. While he's distracted, Molly kicks the ball closer to him. His legs are so thin now that she marvels at his ability to stand.

He shuffles toward the ball and then moves astride to it. "Man, these greens are fast, huh, guys? They must have just cut and rolled 'em. Okay, you're away, Joe." He waits, judging the distance to the cup, while the imaginary Joe takes his turn.

"Good one, Joe. That's a par, right?" He laughs as he sets up to put. "Yep, par for the course." He wavers a bit for balance, peers at the hole he's aiming for, and reminds himself to "Follow through, Liam. Come on."

This time, he has much more control and just taps the ball, which rolls directly to the cup and falls into the hole.

"Great shot, Dad!" Callie grabs his thin forearm to steady him. "You made a par, too!"

"No, no, guys, that was a birdie! I was on in regulation, remember. Haven't had a bird in a while."

Liam speaks to his other golf buddy. "Harry, looks like you're out." Then he whispers to Molly, "He never could putt a damn." Molly nods. "And he cheats. You watch him, see him nudge that ball closer to the hole. "Christ, Harry, will you just putt the damn ball!" Liam glances at Callie. "'Bout time. Okay, is it my turn?" And again, he taps the ball. Miraculously, it also sinks into the hole.

"You still have the touch," Molly says.

"Darn right, George," he answers. "I can't hit a drive, but my short game is my bread and butter." He winks at Molly.

This goes on for ten minutes. Molly smiles at the thought of how much pleasure her father is experiencing, but with each putt, he weakens noticeably. "Dad, you look like you're getting tired," she says.

Liam lets out a sigh. "What's that?"

Callie moves closer to Liam's hearing aid and speaks loudly enough for him to hear her. "Maybe the guys want to call it a day."

"Oh. Oh, yeah, sure. If you guys are tuckered out, we can head up to the clubhouse and get a beer. My treat." Liam drops his putter near his golf ball and reaches for his walker. He stumbles, then steadies himself. He heads toward the bench they sat on earlier, the sisters at his side and the aide watching from several feet away.

He pivots so he can sit, but the walker bumps against the bench, and Liam loses his balance and tips forward toward the bench. Callie grabs his arm, but that just twists him even more, and he starts to fall. Molly is blocked by the walker and can't get to him, and Callie is left hanging on to his arm and his rib cage, but she can't stop his descent. The aide, a young woman, reaches forward in an attempt to cradle his head.

None of them can stop the side of his head from banging into the bench.

"Oh, no!" Molly cries. Everyone is holding on to him and trying to lift and turn him so that his weight is balanced on the bench. Liam does not speak, but his grunt is enough to scare all concerned.

Finally, after the three of them reposition themselves, they have him sitting up. He is breathing hard.

"Should we call the nurse? Get a wheelchair?" But Molly can see that the aide is already heading for help. Callie is now grasping her father's shoulders. "Daddy, can you hear me? Squeeze my hand if you can, okay?" He doesn't; nor does he react in any way. "Oh, God, Molly. We just couldn't hold him."

"Callie, it's not your fault or mine. He's just very weak. Oh look, there's blood on his neck!"

Callie turns Liam's head gently and spots a gash. "He's got a cut under his earlobe. Do you have a tissue? I can stop it if I can put pressure on it, maybe."

Molly drops her purse off her shoulder and pulls out a packet of tissues, grabs a handful, and pushes them at her sister.

"He takes blood thinners, so it's hard to stop any bleeding ... okay ... okay, I think I can at least ... look at his neck."

"Is that the only cut?" Molly asks.

"Well, I think so. Damn it! The blood makes it hard to know for sure. Look, here comes Laurie." Callie uses the tissues to soak up the blood, which keeps dripping down her father's neck onto his shirt.

The nurse has gauze pads, which she uses to staunch the flow of blood, and within minutes, Liam is stabilized. "Good work, ladies. I'm glad you didn't panic, and you stopped most of the bleeding quickly."

Liam suddenly is alert. "What the hell? Hey, who pushed me over?"

Laurie gets down to Liam's eye level so he'll focus on her instead of "Harry" or "George." "Mr. O'Toole, it's me, Nurse Laurie. Can you nod to me so I know you hear me?" He does. "Good. Good. You are fine. Your daughters are here. You just tripped and bumped your head. Do you understand?"

"Um. I fell?"

Molly sees confusion change to guilt in her father's expression as he looks up at her and Callie. "Oh, gosh, girls. I'm sorry I scared you. Wait. I think I cut myself. I see some blood on my shirt."

"That's okay," Laurie reassures him. I bandaged you. We'll see if you need a stitch or two. Your girls caught you when you fell. Lucky for you, they were here helping you, huh?"

Liam nods. "Yes. Yes. Oh, girls, you don't need to fuss. It's just a scrape, probably. Just rub a little dirt on it!" Liam laughs.

They all do. Nervous laughter.

"Just get me back home, girls, and your mother will take care of me ... after she scolds me for not watching where I'm going."

Smiles all around, followed by frowns. The group gets Liam into a wheelchair that the aide has brought and wheels him to his room. Laurie takes some time to clean up his wound properly and take his blood pressure while Callie gets him a clean shirt and helps him into it. Molly then helps him into his recliner and puts a blanket over him.

Laurie advises the sisters, "Let's let him rest a bit before I examine him more closely. Before she can finish the sentence, Liam is snoring.

## Act 2, Scene 5:
# The Importance of Being Alan

Alan stands on an eight-foot ladder gluing the last piece of wallpaper over a faux fireplace in a Victorian drawing room. This is Algernon Moncrieff's house—at least on stage. Alan and Patrick are creating a new set for La Paloma's upcoming production of Oscar Wilde's comedy farce *The Importance of Being Earnest.*

Patrick is taking two cans of yellow and brown paint back to the storage room after painting the backdrop for the third act. Paint is splattered on his white overalls, making them appear to be a design by Jackson Pollock.

Alan grins at the thought of Pollack shocking the mid-1900s art world by heaving dripping paint cans at a canvas, and Moncrieff, a dashing dandy from the late 1800s, doing his best to disrupt Victorian society.

Algernon Moncrieff, a man-about-town, claims to be Earnest because he finds that his latest love interest, Cecily Cardew, whom he has never met, has exchanged a message of love from a gentleman who claims to be Earnest. Algernon pretends to be Cecily's Earnest, hoping to capture her heart. When another Earnest enters the play, both young suitors must admit their guilt. What ensues is a confusing and hilarious portrayal of the absurdity of Victorian society's obsession with appearances and the pursuit of marriage.

Alan makes his way down the ladder to fetch a brush used in the final step of ensuring that the wallpaper stays on the wall. The day has been up the ladder, down the ladder, and up the ladder again. Since helping to tear down the set for the last play, Alan has learned that it's much easier and quicker to tear down a set, or as Patrick calls it *strike* a set, than to design and create a new one.

Patrick steadies the ladder as Alan climbs back up with the brush. He says, "I'm not sure you knew what you were getting into when you agreed to help."

"I didn't know," Alan replies. He brushes the wallpaper to ensure it will adhere perfectly to the plywood so no bubbles will develop. "I keep stepping back to take in the whole set, and I'm impressed with the illusion we've created. It's remarkable." He steps down from the ladder once again, catching his breath. "Okay. I think that's the last of it. I have to say, wallpaper is a pain in the ass, but it gives more depth to the room. I'm just glad we didn't paper the entire room!"

Several members of the crew are milling around Alan and Patrick, adjusting the lighting, marking the floor with tape for blocking, and discussing the placement of the furniture.

"I think that would have been too costly, and the crew would have mutinied." A number of the crew nod at Patrick's remark. He steps back next to Alan, and they gaze at their work.

"Back in the '80s, when wallpaper was trending, Sophie and I tried to do it ourselves. It almost ended our marriage." Alan smiles at the memory of Sophie. He can speak of her now without the debilitating grief and trauma that have been with him for so long. He can share memories of her with others who loved her without creating an atmosphere of gloom.

"Alan, you and the crew have done a great job with the drawing room. It's exactly how I imagined it. I'm gonna touch up the backdrop for the scene out in the country field in the next act." Patrick taps the cans of paint to be sure their seals are tight. Then he heads to the backstage store room for other supplies.

Alan is mesmerized by Algernon's drawing room as envisioned by Patrick. He and the crew have been working on all the details for two solid weeks. The furniture is now in place, and the artwork is being tacked onto the walls.

The camaraderie of the *techies,* as they call themselves, has lifted his spirits as well. The crew has the esprit-de-corps often found in people who volunteer for a passion project—something Alan did not see quite as often during his typical workday.

Zoey arrives with four boxes of pizza. She announces, "One cheese, one veggie, two pepperoni." Patrick follows with a case of beer. Someone yells, "Pizza's here!" and seemingly from the woodwork, actors and crew emerge on La Paloma's stage to grab a slice.

Zoey takes in the appearance of the set. "Dad, this is fantastic! You know, I saw this play in college. Your set is a lot like the one I remember."

"We have less space," Patrick says, "but we do make the most out of what we have."

Alan turns to Zoey, "These folks are really the artists. They painted the bookcase with books that look so realistic that I had to walk right up to them to see they weren't real. And they sewed the drapes from leftover fabric."

"Dad, sit down and get off your feet. Let me get you a slice. Relax. When did you get here?" Zoey gives her father a napkin, a paper plate and a pizza slice, and she pops open a can of beer for him.

"Oh. I think about 10:00 this morning. Time flies." He pauses. "Listen." He looks to the stage where the actors have temporarily taken over a small part of the stage and are rehearsing a scene. Alan and Zoey burst out laughing as the actors go through the confusion over who is really Earnest. The play on words is woven into the irony of being *earnest* or being a *liar.*

Zoey asks, "So, Dad, what are you going to do when this show is ready to open?"

"I was going to ask you to come with me to see it!" He laughs. "By now, I practically know the lines."

"You think you'd ever be up there on stage?"

"No way." He takes another swig of his beer. "Oh, that hit the spot. Nothing like beer and pizza." He takes Zoey's hand. "But I sure wish your mother could see all this ... all the trappings of her theater."

He ignores her offer of a third slice of pizza. "I gotta stop at two." He gets up gingerly. "Oh, damn. My back does not get along with ladders."

Zoey lets out a sigh. "Mom would have been perfect in this play. She'd be into all the Victorian costumes. And she loved comedies, too. She'd be so proud of you. You're turning into a thespian."

"No. I'm just an old stagehand."

"Ha! You are also a fast learner."

Most of the pizza disappears, and the crew gets back to their final assignments.

Renee appears. "Oh, pizza! Thank goodness, I'm starving. Zoey! What are you doing here? Oh, did you bring us the pizza? Of course you did. You're an angel."

"Thanks, Renee. There's beer, too."

"I'm a red wine girl, but thanks." She takes a bite and then reports the news, "We're selling tickets like hotcakes—isn't that an odd expression? Anyway, opening night is sold out, but

I saved two seats for you, Alan, unless you're superstitious about things like opening night."

"Oh. Um. I think I'll go the second week. I'm sure everyone will be nervous the first week." Alan looks at Zoey, who nods in response.

Renee doesn't argue. "True. By week two, we've usually worked out the kinks. However, with this cast, I'm not sure there will be any flubs."

Alan agrees. "They've been off book for over a week." He slaps his head. "Listen to me. I sound like I know what I'm talking about. *Off book.* Crazy."

"Not crazy at all. You'd be a natural up there, counselor." Renee winks at Zoey.

"Oh, don't start on me. That train left the station back in high school when I joined the debate team and decided I wanted to be the valedictorian, so I had to get all A grades. No. I was probably foolish then ... and now. But I won't be heading down that track, Miss Renee."

Renee shrugs. "Oh, well. Our loss. Ah! That reminds me. Patrick was just telling me about his 40th high school reunion that's coming up in October. He's still close to lots of his high school friends. A few of them are patrons of ours."

Renee takes a bite of pizza, and Alan hands her a napkin. "Interesting. My 40th was a few years ago, but it was back East, and I really hadn't stayed connected with my friends except for a few on Facebook. I only went to my 10th reunion. No regrets, though."

Renee takes another bite. She wants to say something but is far too dignified to speak and chew at the same time. She swallows. "You told me you'd talked to Tom Kent about helping us here, right?"

Alan nods.

"You know that Tom was one of Patrick's high school buddies. Right?

"Yes. Tom told me they graduated the same year."

"That's right. You know Tom married his high school sweetheart ... Carol ... is that her name?" Renee finishes her slice of pizza.

Alan politely corrects her. "Callie. Tom and Callie." Alan points to the pizza. "Would you like another slice?"

Renee indicates she is fine as is.

Alan continues. "Sophie and I got together with them many times over the years. I still play basketball at the YMCA with Tom, at least when my back isn't acting up. Ladders are my nemesis."

"Patrick is excited about their 40th high school reunion. He told me that Tom and Callie are going. She's a year younger, but she knows lots of the people in the class of '83." Renee pauses. "Alan, did you know Callie has a twin sister?"

"Hmm. I think Tom mentioned his sister-in-law." Alan stretches his back. "My back isn't what it used to be. And it used to be not so great even then."

Renee nods but stays on point. "Here's the interesting thing. Patrick told me that Callie's sister is Molly O'Toole. You know, the actress."

"Oh. No. I don't know her."

"Well, she was on Broadway back in the '90s, and she's been in lots of television shows. I've followed her for a while because Patrick always mentioned her, being that they went to the same high school. I have no idea if she's in town, but if she is, Patrick is hoping she comes to the 40th reunion. He hasn't seen her in decades. Back in high school, they were in drama together." Renee wipes the pizza grease from her hands. "I surmise that my Patrick had a crush on her." She smiles and rolls her eyes.

Zoey interrupts. "Dad, I gotta go. I'll call you tomorrow before my flight to Denver. I have depositions to do, but I'll be back the same day. If you can pick me up at the airport, I'll treat you to dinner."

"Sure. No problem."

"Thanks. Bye." She kisses him quickly. "See you, Renee. Everything looks great here."

"And my daughter exits stage left. I'm getting the drama lingo down, Renee." Alan reaches for his phone in his back pocket. "You know, now that you mention it, Tom did tell me Callie has a twin sister. I just can't remember—or I forgot—you know, another senior moment—that she was an actres*s*. What did you say her name was? Molly O ... what?"

"O'Toole. With an apostrophe."

Alan taps the Google icon and types the name.

## Act 2, Scene 6:
# The Bocce Ball Boys

Molly is now free from an actress's starvation diet. Nevertheless, a dinner roll with butter equals a long walk-workout with a well-deserved rest afterward on a bench near the bocce ball sand pit in Ameci Park.

Four octogenarian men nearby are arguing in Italian about whose ball is closest to the *pallino*. Hands are flying in every direction, index fingers are pointing accusingly at chests, and voices are getting louder and louder. Molly smiles at their antics, knowing that bocce ball requires agreement on which team has landed their ball closest to the *pallino*.

One of them, the one wearing a black fedora with a red feather tucked into the brim, looks up at her with an expression she doesn't need to understand Italian to read: *whata ya gonna do?*

Another man, this one bald with a silver goatee, looks away from the argument and spots the source of his companion's attention: a strikingly attractive woman on a nearby bench who seems to be laughing at them. He stares and then calls out, "*Signora. Signora.* We need you help here. Please come! Come here!"

Molly turns slightly away from the group. She does not want to get involved in an argument about whose ball has been thrown closer to the target ball.

The two other men in the foursome, one clean-shaven and wearing oversized black sunglasses, and the other looking as if he needed a shave yesterday, take note of the distraction and stop arguing. The man in the black fedora hat pleads, "*Donna bellissima.* Please. *Signora,* we need your eyes. These two can't see. They cheat!"

Molly knows that these four men are much more interested in flirting with her than they are in judging the game. Grudgingly, she rises from her perch. *After all, they did compliment me.* She strolls leisurely towards them. Black Fedora and Silver Goatee smile wider. The other two do not seem pleased that *she* might settle their argument.

Molly takes her time crossing the 20 or so feet to them, making sure not to notice that Black Fedora and Silver Goatee are tucking in their shirts and sucking in their pot bellies while Black Sunglasses and Five-O'Clock Shadow are stone-faced.

"*Buongiorno, Signores*," she says from five feet away. "What is the matter?"

And with this question, like the starter's gun being fired at the races, an uproar begins. All four of them are yelling and pleading at the same time, clamoring in a mashup of Italian and English about the travesty of injustice that has befallen them in their game.

After a last volley of words, Black Sunglasses shouts, "*Aspetta!*" The other men stop, as if this man has some power over them that Molly does not quite fathom. He composes himself and speaks to Molly, "*Signora,* do you speak Italian?"

"Just a little. I know that your friend called me a *beautiful woman.*"

He bows his head in apology for them being too forward. This gives Five O'Clock Shadow the opportunity to enter the conversation: "Geno is right, *Signora.* But we should call you by your name. We don't know you, eh?"

"Oh, well. I'm flattered. Geno, my name is Molly. That is followed by a chorus of "Ah, Molly!"

"What she say?" asks Black Fedora.

"*Molly!* What's the matter with you? Can't you hear her!" Geno hits Black Fedora in the back of his head, tilting his hat over his face. He tells her, "You know we all don't hear like we used to ... when we used to."

"You sound stupid," Five O'clock Shadow tells Geno.

"Don't call me stupid. At least I can see whose ball is closer."

Mr. Black Sunglasses cuts to the chase. "Shut up. Okay. *Signora*, whose ball is closer to the little ball? Huh? The red one or the green one?"

"You need to look close." Black Fedora bends over to show her just how it is done.

Molly interrupts the judging. "Wait. Wait. You know my name, but other than Geno and his silver goatee, what are your names?"

Black Sunglasses again takes charge. "Oh, so sorry. I'm Sergio. My brother, who never shaves, is Rudy. This one with the hat, he is Big Sal. We call him that because he has the biggest head ever. And Geno is the one who called you beautiful. Which you are. Okay?"

Rudy steps closer to Molly. "Now, we are not gonna tell you whose ball is whose, okay? Why? Because you would pick the color of the team that is the better-looking team. Like me and Sergio, for sure. But we don't want you prejudiced."

"You are the team full of bullshit," Geno parries.

Sergio quiets the quartet. "Molly, you decide. I trust you. Besides, we are all old enough to be your papa. And we are also *equally* ugly."

"Sergio, you are making me blush. I'm not so young."

Big Sal proclaims, "She reminds me of the actress, Sophia Loren, no?"

"Shut up!" Rudy pokes at his mortal bocce ball enemy, "She no have black hair like Sophia Loren, and she is ... smaller."

Molly understands Rudy's gesture, referring to her bosom. They all chuckle. Then she comes back with, "Okay, let me see your balls."

They howl with laughter. Big Sal doubles over, and Molly is slightly concerned she may have given him a heart attack.

Sergio again brings quiet to the group. Molly looks at him, "Sergio, these guys all listen to you. How come?"

"He was a priest!" Big Sal says while gasping for breath. "But he quit."

"Because my brother saw Sophia Loren!" Rudy ignites more laughter.

"And that was that!" Geno concludes.

Molly decides it is time to get down to business. She leans over the bocce balls and looks closely. The four men lean closer to her, too. She deliberately walks around the balls, sizing up the distance going north, south, east, and west. The men follow, obviously appreciating her ... diligence.

"I say it's ... it's a tie!" Molly beams.

"No. No. No. It can't be!" Geno's hands slap his forehead.

"You boys need to have a do-over."

They argue for a few seconds, but then Rudy tells her, "Only if you stay and watch."

"Sorry, boys, I'll see you next week. I have an appointment at the beauty salon."

Big Sal makes a big gesture. "Why? You are already *Bella Donna!*"

"*Grazie, prego,* boys. *Caio!*" Molly waves as she walks away.

As she heads back to her condo to get ready for her appointment at the hair salon, Callie calls about meeting her afterwards. Molly regales her with the short version of her playful adventure with the old Italian men.

"Be careful, Molly. Remember what Carmen told you at the restaurant. They will keep pestering you."

Molly stops walking and sits by the fountain in the piazza, "Oh, Callie. I was just having fun with them." She sighs, looking into the water bubbling up. It reminds her of the song "Three Coins in the Fountain."

The two are quiet for a moment. Then, Molly explains, "Believe me, I am not searching for a man to find happiness. If I have learned anything in my 59 years, it's that I have to work on myself and what makes me feel alive and joyful. It can't just be playing parts in make-believe films. I want to be Molly O'Toole and only Molly O'Toole. Not some damsel in distress. Believe me, men have been the source of too much pain and disappointment."

It's a few seconds before Callie reminds her, "At least the ones you've chosen, Molly."

"You're right. I know. Bad choices. Impulsive. I've let loneliness get to me." As she stands, Molly sees all the coins that have been tossed in the fountain. "Okay, thanks for listening, Callie. I love you. I'll see you later." Molly walks away, the song's lyrics floating somewhere nearby. She wonders how many lovers have been blessed when they tossed coins into this fountain. She reaches into her purse and finds a quarter and, just for luck, tosses it into the bubbling water.

## Act 2 Scene 7:
# The Flawless Touch

"Let's meet at the coffee shop next to the salon, okay?" Molly asks her sister. Then she replies, slightly annoyed, "No, I'm not coloring my hair ever again. Those days are over." Molly waits for the crossing light to blink green while she continues her phone call. "And, no, I am just getting a trim. Yes, yes. The Flawless Touch. Right. Yes, that's the place on the corner of E Street."

She crosses Highway 101 along with an oblivious gaggle of teenage girls screaming at each other about boys while they parade through downtown in their bathing suits. It's September, and the surf is up. Molly remembers doing the same thing when she was 16 years old—only with slightly less skin showing.

On the opposite corner, she stops suddenly. "Callie, this is the same place we used to go to years ago. Yeah, it had a different name, but my Little Italy guide, Gia— remember I told you about her—anyway, Gia recommended it and told me to ask for Renee, the new owner."

She peers in the front window to take in the vibe. "Remember ... wait ... what? What do you mean Renee is married to Patrick?" She turns her back to the salon's entrance, worried that this Renee person might overhear her. She's aware that salon gossip can penetrate glass and even brick walls. "Are you talking about the Patrick we knew in high school? No way. Can't be. You and Tom hang out with them? Why didn't you ever tell me this? Patrick Sorenson! Yeah, the same guy in my drama class. Shit. He used to have a huge crush on me. Yes, of course I'm serious!"

Molly peeks into the salon. "Well, this may be awkward. Do you like Renee? Okay, well. That's great. I'm glad she and Patrick have been married all these years. It says a lot about her ... and him. But she must know who I am and about how Patrick and I used to hang out." Molly listens to Callie, then whispers as if everyone is listening to their phone chatter, "What are you implying? No! We didn't *do it!* For Christ's sake, Callie. I was a virgin until ... oh, shut up. We just made out. Look, I'll be at the coffee place ..." She looks down the street. "The Better Buzz. Yeah. See you in an hour. Yeah. Okay, bye." Molly drops her phone into her oversized purse. She takes a big breath, puts on a big smile, and enters as gracefully as ... as an actress.

The Flawless Touch is the last of the storefronts on this 1930s-style red brick block stretching from D to E Street. The stores are a mix of funky and old school. There are the Coast Highway Traders, selling Bohemian-style clothing and locally designed jewelry; Bliss 101, which sells artwork and furnishings created by San Diegans; Flashbacks, dealing in retro and recycled clothing; and several bars. One of them, The Daley Double Saloon, is a historic night spot with live music and a burly security guy sitting shotgun, just in case things get out of hand.

Renee's salon was a bit of a drive for Molly, but she'd planned on meeting Callie after her trim, and Gia had been so enthusiastic about it. So, she'd figured the drive would be worth it. She remains particular about her hair even though she's given up acting. Hair obsessiveness is a hard habit to change.

Inside, The Flawless Touch has an artsy feel. Molly sees pictures of sunsets, two surfboards painted with wave designs, and photos of tanned, gorgeous fashion models adorning baby-blue walls. The salon is bright and cheerful, and a plaque on the wall behind the receptionist's counter boasts that it's even green-certified. There's music, a blend of Jamaican reggae and hip hop. Behind the receptionist's area, there are seven chairs with young girls cutting, coloring, and in one booth, manicuring.

Molly spies a woman in the back who appears to be in her fifties, decades senior to the other women tending to customers. This must be Renee.

Renee is elegant. Her long brown hair is feathered down across her left shoulder, the right side cropped closer with a thin braid coming across her right ear. Molly realizes her style is very beachy, far from her more traditional shoulder-length and parted-down-the-middle with bangs look. She wonders if she's frumpy compared to Patrick's wife.

"You must be Molly!" Renee extends her hand. It is warm and inviting.

"Yes. And you are Renee, I assume. Gia's told me you're the best."

"Oh, thank you. I just had Gia here last week. She told me she recommended me to you. I feel I know you already because my husband, Patrick, talks about you. *Molly O'Toole*, he says, the famous actress he knew in high school." Renee guides Molly to her chair—the first one right by the window—a place reserved for the proprietor. "Please, let me take your purse. I want you to just relax."

"Renee, you are being so kind, but I am not famous ... maybe I'm infamous. And I am now just a retired actress. I'm done with Hollywood and L.A. I just recently moved down here to be near my sister and my father. It's taking a while, but I'm starting to feel like I'm home again after many years."

Molly sits back in the chair and tries to do as Renee insists: relax. "You know, my sister, Callie, and I used to come here, I think before you bought the place. By the way, I love the vibe. And she and I both came here when we were in our twenties to get our hair done."

"Yes. I was fortunate to have partners who helped me get started here. They left me for their children and families, but by the time they did, I was on solid ground with a strong base of clients. And, of course, then I met Patrick. We discovered we are soulmates, both part of the same artistic tribe, you know what I mean?"

Molly nods, "Oh, I understand. I spent much of my life, my career, with creative people." *I like her.*

"Patrick had his own music business and, well, one thing led to another and whoosh, we've been married twenty-five years."

Molly senses that Renee seems secure in her relationship with Patrick, and her nervousness abates. This is a woman who is, like her, fierce and empowered. At least, like she used to be. She's envious but pushes that away. "And I've been acting for forty years. When I think of that, it makes my head spin."

Molly lets a moment pass to consider how she wants to reference Patrick. "I remember Patrick. He was in drama with me. He was a good actor, but I always knew his passion was music. Guitar, as I recall. He would play for us during boring rehearsals."

Renee and Molly are communicating through the reflection in the mirror as Renee runs her hands through Molly's hair. It is a sensual, bonding experience between two women who just seem to click. "Oh, Patrick! When I told him you were coming in to have your hair done, I thought he was going to come down here from the theater to get your autograph. I told him, 'Forget it, Mister!' You are not going to embarrass her in my salon." Renee disengages and reaches back for the salon cape.

"Thank you, Renee," Molly whispers. "I'm sure we all will get together soon."

Renee drapes a salon cape on Molly, securing it around her neck. "Are you staying with your sister in Encinitas?"

"No. Right now, I'm staying in Little Italy for a while until I find something around here."

"Good. Good. Take your time. San Diego is, as you must know, very mellow compared to Los Angeles. Let's go wash your gorgeous hair. Okay?"

They chat about each other's interests and what it's like to reach certain milestones in their careers as businesswomen. Once back in the chair, Molly tells Renee she just wants a trim and that she is no longer going to color her hair. "I'm very lucky my hair is still healthy, considering all the crazy things acting has caused me to do to it. You can imagine."

Renee nods. "Yes. Your hair just shimmers. I love it. For now, just a nice trim. Maybe later we can do some fun things with it, eh?" She smiles.

"You said Patrick is working at the theater. What does he do?"

"Oh, gosh. I should explain. We own the La Paloma Playhouse. We restored it in 2002 from an old movie theater. It took us ten years. We've been at it for over a decade. Patrick loves it. It's his passion."

"You're kidding. Wow. I remember going to see surfing movies there when we were kids. It was pretty funky back then. I'll have to check it out."

"Oh, I'm afraid Patrick will insist."

"Do you think my hair will come out iron gray? I hope not. I wish it would be white, like Callie's. But she was always blonde, so maybe that figures. Considering all the chemicals and dyes I used, who knows? Anyway, I was born with red hair."

"We shall find out together. I imagine, whatever your style and color, you'll always turn heads. Which makes me wonder, did you move down here alone, or do you have a partner or a man in your life? If you don't mind me asking."

Molly shakes her head, "No. I'm single and on my own. I left men and the drama of dating back in L.A. My only flirtations are with the old Italian men who play bocce ball." She laughs, and Renee smiles.

"If you change your mind, you know we women here in the salon know some very appealing men. And which men to avoid like the plague."

"Good to know, Renee. I'm not really in the market for a man now. I'm just focusing on me, myself and I. You know, I've played so many women in my life, but the woman I need to rediscover is me. I hope you don't think I'm being too dramatic, but this is a chance for me to trust myself and ... and love who I am." Molly looks directly up at Renee through the reflection in the mirror. Renee stops what she is doing. They both stay quiet momentarily.

Then, Renee's face subtly transforms from that of a hairdresser to a confidant. She bends close to Molly's ear, "You are stronger than you know. I was there. I still am. We can do this, believe me."

Molly's throat tightens, and her eyes water, though she quickly draws back from the emotion. She smiles at Renee, who squeezes her shoulders and continues with her scissors and styling.

"However," Molly says, "I will make sure I check with you first when and if I change my mind ... about men, I mean."

Other topics breeze by like the cars cruising down Highway 101 as Renee blow dries Molly's hair and then turns her chair so she's once again looking in the mirror. "Molly, are you going to the 40th reunion of your high school this fall? Patrick is all excited about it."

"Oh. No. He was in the class before me."

"Yes, but your sister is going. Her husband is in Patrick's class."

"Oh. Really. Tom. Hmm. That's right. Well, that's very interesting. I wonder why my sister didn't tell me about this."

Renee touches Molly's shoulders. "Well, I hope you go. It'll be fun. You and your sister, and Tom and Patrick and me. But even if you don't go, you're going to have fun here, small town and all. Patrick and I went to the 30th, and that year they had a band. We danced. God, I hadn't danced in years."

"Renee, I don't know. Wow. I'm not sure I should go. Dancing. Yikes! All I know is slow dancing ... and that has always gotten me in trouble." They both laugh.

Renee finishes by styling Molly's hair the way she always likes it. "Let's consider blending in the gray as it comes in, okay? Does that appeal to you?"

"I think that's exactly what I would love. Thank you, Renee."

As Molly stands to pay Renee, she says, "I'll think about going to the reunion. I'm meeting my sister next door for coffee. I'll have to ask her why she hasn't mentioned it. Bye, Renee. I hope we see each other socially."

"I'm sure we will." They give each other a quick hug.

As Molly strolls down Main Street, she ponders the question Renee raised: Do you have a boyfriend or a partner? In her old Hollywood days, she would have had a string of men whom she could socialize with—and some of them were "friends with benefits"—but relationships like that were sure to turn sour, much like her voluptuous red hair fading into shades of gray.

She suspects no man has the answers to her questions about her new life. Here I am, she wonders: new town, no job, no floodlights, no relationship. Am I just another woman with iron gray hair? Am I really done with men?

She pauses for an instant and unexpectedly catches her breath. The thought of having to find the answers to these questions herself thrills her.

## Act 2, Scene 8:
# The Phone Call

"So, it's decided, then. You're not going." Callie sounds disappointed, even though she's known Molly's intention.

"Right. Like I tried to tell you, Callie. It's not because you didn't tell me—you may have assumed I'd go—but like I said, it's not my scene. Maybe next year for *our* reunion. I really wouldn't know anyone other than Patrick and Renee. But ..."

"But what?" Callie is laying out her fashion choices for the evening while her phone is on speaker.

"But I promised Renee I'd go to the theater to see Patrick before you guys head to the reunion. I know you all are meeting there first for a drink."

"Oh, right. They have a show that night, and they wanted Patrick to be at the theater to make sure everything goes off right."

Molly explains, "So, I'll get there at 6:30 when you're meeting."

"Okay. Okay. I get it, but ..."

"Another but?"

"But you gotta promise me that for our 40th reunion ... "

Molly stops her. She knows she cannot let her sister down. *A promise is a promise.* "Oh, all right, you! I am *in* for next year."

Now, Molly is also looking through her wardrobe. Twins tend to think alike. "What are you wearing?" She has one hand on the stem of her glass of white wine and the other moving the hangers in the closet.

"Funny you should ask. At Tom's 20th reunion, lots of women were dressed to party with *I'm a hot bitch* look. Boobs hanging out, short skirts ..."

"Real boobs?"

"I doubt it," Callie says. "They looked quite top-heavy. They were into whiskey or tequila. Hard stuff. All into impressing and flirting. Then, ten years ago at Tom's 30th, women were dressed to impress. Less skin showing, more wrinkles, some who clearly had work done. And it was a white wine affair."

"Ah ha! Plastic surgeons were busy."

"Yep. Black dresses, knee length, hair colored. Of course, this was before COVID, and naturally, for some, divorces were justified, yada yada. The flirting was less about sex and more about bragging about how successful they were. The ones who were not into success in business were talking about their kids. I found them far more enjoyable."

Molly interrupts. "Those are some of the other reasons not to go." She chooses black jeans and a purple button-up top with a string of petite cultured pearls to accessorize. "But I am really looking forward to seeing Patrick again. And Renee told me about all the work they've done to the theater since they bought the building." She heads to the fridge to add another splash of wine to her glass. "We had lunch together, Renee and I, and like you, Callie, she has her life together. You two inspire me."

"Well, thank you. I really haven't gotten to know Renee. I'm glad you have. And, for sure, the La Paloma is so much nicer. It was on the verge of being bulldozed. Then COVID hit them, and they just barely were hanging on, I heard. Hmm." Callie is still rummaging through her closet. "Dress choice. Should I go with blue or black? Whadda ya think?"

Molly moves to the living room couch. "Oh. I don't know. Blue? They were lucky to survive COVID. In my world, it wiped out theaters, actors, and crew members. It was a freaking nightmare. I knew two actors from the East Coast who passed away. Anyway, bad memories." She decides to change the tone of the conversation, "But thankfully, the La Paloma survived. You know, I saw the marquee the other day. They're producing one of my favorite plays, *The Importance of Being Earnest*. It'll be interesting to see if they can pull it off."

"Okay, blue," Callie responds, "and pearls. Oh, are you planning on staying to see the play after we head out?"

"No, no."

Molly hears the familiar sound of fear in her own voice. So many years of auditions. So many rejections. Too many unwanted advances, several causing scars that remain invisible to the naked eye. Anything having to do with theater is now difficult for her.

Callie asks, "What are you going to do, then?"

"I'm going to dinner and a movie."

"Alone?" Callie sounds worried.

"Yeah. Is that a problem?" Molly knows exactly what her sister is thinking.

"Well, no. Not really."

"I'm perfectly comfortable being *me*. Callie, I've decided that this new chapter of my life is about what *I* want to do, who *I* want to be. A better, independent me. Did you know, for example, that Leo has called me at least four times, leaving messages?" Molly reclines on her couch, legs outstretched, and yawns.

"What does he say?"

"I don't know. He leaves voicemails, and I don't listen. I don't want to listen because I am not going back to that life." Molly adjusts her head on a throw pillow, pivots, and swings her legs up on the pillow at the far end of the couch. "I haven't even had a chance to breathe." Molly lets out a long sigh. "Believe me, Sis. What you and Tom have is beautiful. You two have been together so long, but you each have your own space."

Callie walks to the fridge to get a glass of wine. "I understand. Well, I don't really because it's always been me and Tommy."

"While I had Kurt and then a bunch of pretenders. Maybe I was like them for a while ... for far too long. I was always looking over my shoulder for the next big thing. A part in a play, a new leading man, a bigger spotlight. Now, I'm trying to stop looking around. I'm trying to focus on myself for once." Molly closes her eyes and relaxes into the softness of her new couch.

Callie pours chilled chardonnay into a goblet. "Molly, look. I know you are my big sister by four minutes, but you have always been my heroine on screen and in real life."

They are quiet. A minute passes. Molly looks at her watch. "Shit. Look at the time! I gotta get ready! *You really* gotta get ready! Love you."

"Love you back."

## Act 2, Scene 9:
# When Alan Met Molly

Alan looks in the mirror. Following Patrick's advice, he is wearing black because that is what the backstage crew wears to disappear from the audience's view during the play's scene changes. Zoey is meeting him at the theater because, on this third Saturday performance, he and Zoey are filling in for Patrick and Renee, who are attending the evening's reunion.

The day before, Alan and Patrick ran through what he needed to do. Zoey will take over Renee's duties at the ticket booth, provide intermission refreshments, and see to any wardrobe malfunctions. Alan will be moving set pieces before each act. *The Importance of Being Earnest* is a successful play at the La Paloma Playhouse, he told Patrick. "Don't worry. I won't screw it up."

Alan values punctuality, so he arrives thirty minutes before Zoey and most of the actors. He feels like a lost sheep waiting to be found. He hears some backstage noises and an occasional crash against something unidentified, but otherwise, all is quiet on the theater front.

He enters the back of the theater, takes in the overall look of the stage and smiles. The illusion of a Victorian parlor is remarkable. A stage door opens to the parlor, and Patrick appears. "Ah, Alan! You're here. Great."

"Look at you, Patrick. Suit and bow tie! Looking very dapper." Patrick hops down from the set, and they meet in the main aisle and shake hands. "I'm at your service," Alan bows.

"Renee and I could not be in better hands. And if anything crazy happens and someone decides to sue us, well, then my lawyer is already on the scene!"

"Oh, God. Let's not even kid about that." Alan waves his right hand toward the seats, "I see you're sold out tonight. The play has become the talk of the town."

"Yes. We hoped *Earnest* would draw big crowds. People love comedy, and Oscar Wilde delivers every time. I chatted backstage with the stage manager and reminded her that you're working on two scene changes. Of course, she already knows—she's always on top of things. You can check in with her later. I think Renee is almost ready, and we expect Tom and Callie will be here soon ... and I hope Molly O'Toole has decided to join us."

Alan looks away from the set and back to Patrick. "Ah, yes. Renee mentioned her. A Broadway actress as a high school alumnus. You two shared the stage back in the day, huh?"

"Well, let's just say we were *standing* on the same stage," Patrick chuckles. "Molly was the actress. I was the crew, just like I am today. That reminds me, I need to check on a light we moved. Make sure it's on the correct circuit. I'll be right back."

Patrick heads up the stairs to the catwalk just as Renee calls from the lobby, "Alan, is that you that I hear?" Alan retraces his steps and meets Renee by the ticket counter in the lobby. Renee is wearing a ruby red dress with black accessories, and her hair is in a French braid.

Alan strides up to her and gives her a warm hug. "You look like a regular stagehand, Alan," she says.

"And you look like a French movie star," he replies. "As for me. I'm just part of the crew. I hope I don't mess up my small part tonight." Alan looks up to see Zoey opening the front door.

"Zoey!" Renee turns to her and they embrace. "I'm so glad you can help your father tonight, not that he needs it. Patrick and I are relieved you can cover for me."

Zoey removes her jean jacket and rubs her hands together. "This is exciting, Renee. I am so happy to not be doing something that involves the law." She hugs her father. "I pulled up next to Callie and Tom. They should be here in a minute. Are you excited to be at the reunion?"

Renee shrugs her shoulders. "This is Patrick's thing. I know he's really looking forward to it. He schmoozes quite a bit, and he has friends he hasn't seen since ... well, since the last reunion ten years ago. Let me show you the ticket situation and where the refreshments are for intermission." She takes Zoey's hand and leads her away.

Alan shoves his hands into his pockets. He doesn't like not having something to do. He knows that this is the calm before the storm, when the lobby will be wall-to-wall people. He checks his watch and then turns to see Tom holding the lobby door open for Callie and another woman, whom he assumes is Callie's sister, Molly. *So that's Molly O'Toole.*

"Alan!" Tom calls. "I heard you were going to be here tonight. Patrick has roped you into theater duty. All in black, I see. You're not playing a priest, I hope."

Alan and Tom jostle, wrapping their arms around each other's shoulders. "All for a good cause," Alan replies.

Callie chimes in. "Alan, it's so nice to see you here. Is that Zoey over with Renee?"

"Yes. She's here to make sure I don't screw up."

Tom cuts in, "Alan, I've been rude. Let me introduce you to Callie's twin sister, Molly."

Alan stands a foot taller than Molly, who has stepped forward and is extending her hand to him. He takes her hand in his and says, "Hello. It is a pleasure to meet you, Molly." Pointing his thumb at Tom, he continues, "I've been palling around with this guy for the last decade or so. And that's my daughter, Zoey, with Renee." Zoey overhears her name and looks up to wave at the four of them.

"Alan, it's my pleasure to meet you. Anyone who can put up with Callie's Tom has to be a good guy. You're dressed for the backstage, I see. Are you in the play? I'm at a disadvantage here. Nobody tells me anything."

Alan suspects Molly knows more than she is revealing. "Oh, no. God forbid. Zoey and I are just here to hold down the fort while you're at the reunion. I'm not ..."

Before he can finish the sentence, Patrick enters the lobby and erupts, "Molly O'Toole! In the flesh!"

"Patrick!" They hold each other at arm's length, taking in the measure of each other.

"Look at you!" Molly exclaims.

"Me! No way. Look at you! Broadway to Hollywood to our little theater. It's been so long. Renee tells me you're here to stay. We have a lot of catching up to do." Patrick steps back, looking confused since, as he can see, Molly is dressed casually. "Wait. You *are* coming to the reunion. Right?

"I'm sorry, Patrick, but your reunion is just not my thing. I promised Callie I would go next year. But we definitely need to catch up." Molly pauses and looks at Renee. "I am so happy for you both. You look terrific." Molly looks at the couples who surround her. "All of you. I'm sure you'll have a great time."

Patrick nods, "Well, I understand. I imagine there is no changing your mind?"

"Nope. I'm still that stubborn girl you knew way back when." She and Patrick embrace.

Smiles all around. Alan raises his eyebrows, impressed with Molly's resolve. Then, he hears the pop of a cork. Renee and Zoey are filling flutes for a toast. Callie is quick to hand them out to the group. Renee raises hers. "Let's have a toast."

All form a circle and Renee continues, "To tonight. To the Class of '83. And to our great friends, Alan and Zoey, and our newest neighbor, Molly. *Cheers!*" They tap glasses. Small talk follows among the group, and then Callie turns to her sister, "Are you still heading to the movies?"

Molly doesn't appear to hear her sister because she has stepped away toward the door to the stage and is peering in through its small window to see inside. Callie steps closer and repeats the question, and this time Molly hears her.

"Oh, no. I looked, but there's nothing playing I'm interested in. I grabbed a salad earlier." She turns back to Alan, "Alan, are you working with the crew tonight? I think that's what I heard."

Alan steps closer to the door. "Just for this evening. It's a learning experience. However, I should say I am quite proud of the set. After I retired, I was looking for a chance to get involved with the community, and Patrick accepted my offer to help with set construction and such." Hoping that Molly is interested, he asks, "Would you like a quick tour?"

Molly looks at Callie to see if time is an issue. Callie insists, "Go ahead, I'm going to chat with Zoey."

Alan holds the door open, and the two of them enter the back of the theater and move to the center aisle, taking in the interior. Molly touches the back of one of the seats and nods. She looks up at the lighting and seems impressed. Then she walks close to the foot of the stage and peers closely at the parlor belonging to Algernon Moncrieff.

Alan has kept his distance, allowing Molly to get the feel of the old establishment, which has been restored with so much effort. *What does she think? After all, she's been on Broadway.*

She sits down in a seat in the front row. "Alan, this is so impressive. Look at the detail you've all put into the parlor. I love it." Molly twists herself around to spot the booth in the far corner where the lighting and technical effects are cloistered. "Great layout. This is intimate theater at its best. Patrick has made the most out of the space he has here. Fantastic."

Alan watches as she absorbs the feel of the place. "Tom tells me you've given up acting?"

"Yes."

"Do you miss it?" he asks gently.

She stands, straightens herself, turns to Alan and smiles. "I think I will never *not* miss it. "She walks up to him and pivots at the set, "Did you work on this set? Because it is marvelous."

Alan steps a bit closer, "I had a hand in it, yes. That wall there," pointing to the area where the fireplace and bookcase meet, "That's my contribution. Wallpaper is a pain, though."

"Well, it looks so realistic. I want to reach out and grab one of those books," she laughs, "Well done, Mr. Alan."

"Patrick is the designer and mastermind. But thank you."

Callie pokes her head in, "Molly, we're heading out now."

"Okay, I'll be right up." When she gets to the lobby, she asks Renee if there is anything she can do to help with tonight's show.

Renee is surprised but says, "Zoey will likely be overwhelmed at intermission with patrons, so if you feel like staying, that would be great. But don't feel obligated. I mean if you have other plans ..."

Molly cuts her off. "Renee, I don't. I'd love to help. I'll just stand in the back and watch the play. I've always loved *Earnest.*

"You don't need to stand. There's a seat next to the lighting booth where Patrick usually sits."

"Oh, great. I know it's a sellout."

The group is ready to leave. Molly waves to them and quickly hugs her sister. "I hope you have a great time." Then she turns to Zoey, "Hi, I'm Molly. We haven't been introduced, but I know you're Alan's daughter."

Zoey smiles, "Yes. It's so nice to meet you."

"Renee mentioned that intermission will be busy. I told her I can help you, if that's all right with you."

"Oh, please. I barely know where everything is, and there's so little time to serve everyone during an intermission. And that will mean my dad won't be looking over my shoulder." They both smile, knowing what fathers can be like, and head over to the bar to check out what's available.

Her father and the stage manager head backstage to practice the garden scene set change, and just then, the first patrons appear at the door.

Molly looks at Zoey and grins. "It's showtime!"

## Act 2 Scene 10:
# The Intermission

Molly sneaks out of the theater and into the lobby with minutes to spare before intermission begins. She knows this play so well that she knows the intermission is coming. Zoey has set up beverages and snacks in preparation for an onrush of audience members hoping for refreshments. "I'll work the people," she tells Molly, "and you take the money, okay." Molly gives her the thumbs up. Then the doors open and the mad rush begins.

The women make the usual dash for the restrooms, and the men hurry up to Zoey to ask for drinks and snacks. Fifteen minutes of chaos ensues, but the dynamic duo keeps the patrons happy and hydrated. Many of them are chatting about how wonderful *Earnest* has been so far. Molly is not surprised. Then the lights blink, a bell rings, and Alan announces that the play is about to restart. People scurry from the bathrooms, the smokers in the outdoor alley scuttle in, and the lobby's final buyers are vacuumed up and sucked back to their seats.

Zoey and Molly see Alan smile and nod to them as he shuts the doors. "Whew!" they gasp. Molly looks at Zoey, "Renee said to lock the front door so nobody can come in while we deal with the cash and receipts."

"Good idea. I have the keys."

They sort through the money, replace the drinks and the snacks and clean up as if they are a well-oiled machine and not two newbies thrown into the crowd's storm.

Zoey takes her hairbrush from her purse to tend to her hair and turns to Molly. "We make a great team, huh?"

"Damn right." They high-five. Molly applies a fresh coat of lipstick. "Actually, that was fun, and frankly, I don't know how one person could have done it." She puts her lipstick away and tells Zoey, "You are so good with people, Zoey. If you don't mind me asking, what do you do in your day job?"

Zoey laughs. "I deal with pretty demanding people. I'm a lawyer. Following in my father's footsteps."

"Oh, I see. Your father is a lawyer?"

"Yep."

"I imagine that keeps him quite busy."

"Retired. I finally talked some sense into him. He's been a workaholic, and he is now learning to slow down ... a little." Zoey rolls her eyes.

Molly smiles and grabs a chair to get off her feet. "It's nice that you two are close."

Zoey checks her phone out of habit, then, in an instant of self-reproach, realizes that whatever is online isn't as important as engaging with her new coworker. "It's been kinda the way it has to be." She pauses. "Circumstances and all."

Molly wonders what circumstances but doesn't want to appear nosy. "I get that. Circumstances change everything, and sometimes the changes are unavoidable. "Take my sister and me. We've always been close, but with me living in Los Angeles, well, there has always been a canyon that separates us and has drawn Callie closer to our father than I am."

"Oh, he is still alive?"

"Yes. That's the hard thing. He has dementia and is in memory care. That's one of my reasons for moving down here." Molly decides to open up a bit more. "To help her and be with him and spend as much time as I can while he's still with us."

"I'm sure he loves seeing you, both of you, but it must be hard. I really can't imagine." Molly appreciates the truth in Zoey's words. Before seeing her father and his golf game, she couldn't have imagined the sadness that dementia causes families.

Zoey is upbeat, possibly deliberately. "I'm gonna grab a Coke. You want one?"

Molly nods, and Zoey heads to the refrigerator, coming back with two bottles. "Don't you want to see the second act of the play?" she asks.

"Oh, no. I've seen it many times. But the cast is doing a great job. I'd just as soon sit and chat with you, to be honest."

Zoey takes a sip of her Coke. "I heard from Renee that you just retired from acting."

"Retired? Hmm. Well, another way of putting it is 'I just *quit.*" Molly smiles ruefully.

"Oh." Zoey looks surprised. She leans forward as if to say, "Tell me more."

"Retiring sounds better," Molly admits, taking a sip of her Coke. "But the truth is that I'd just had it with the entire business. The acting roles for someone my age just were not ... just not challenging or in any way meaningful." She sighs. Her idealism about being an actress was tarnished long ago, but she has decided to keep certain experiences to herself.

"Oh my. Well, that's understandable." Then after a moment, "Molly, I think what you've decided takes a lot of courage. I know I'm less than ten years into my career, but if I felt as you do, well, I don't know if I could just start over, you know? You're starting a new life here, and that's a big adjustment."

The two sit quietly for a minute. Molly has surprised herself by revealing so much to someone she's just met. She's impressed with Zoey's mature response. She realizes this woman, decades her junior, has a warm-hearted disposition.

The quiet in the lobby is suddenly broken by a roar of laughter from within the theater. The two smile, and Molly nods, "I gather the farce has been exposed!"

Once the laughter dies down, Zoey pulls out a Kit Kat bar from her pocket and looks at Molly, "Wanna split it?"

Molly nods her head enthusiastically. "It's been a while since I had candy. I used to love Kit Kats. And Snickers."

"I'm a dark chocolate Mounds girl," Zoey cracks the bar in half. They both take small bites of the guilty pleasure. "When I was little, my dad and I would sneak out and get ice cream. We didn't tell my mom because she would say that he was spoiling my appetite ... which was true." She takes another bite. "My dad just sort of *quit,* too, like you said. He was a partner in a law firm, and he just kept working because ... because it was habitual. He needed a change. I knew he was bored. And lonely. So, this has been good for him, being here and meeting new people. New challenges."

Molly recognizes that Alan must not be married. "It's just the two of you? No brothers or sisters?"

"Yep. Just two lawyers." Zoey chuckles. "My father was a criminal lawyer, and he was fantastic! I got to watch him in court sometimes when I was a teenager. He commanded the courtroom."

Molly listens intently, like an actress understanding a character's traits. "Funny. He seems very reserved. He told me he'd never act on stage."

"Ah, well. Law was his milieu. He knew his part and loved it. Acting would terrify him, I suppose."

Molly replies, "I played lawyers from time to time. It's easy when your lines are written for you. If you mess up, they cut and redo the scene. How long have you been a lawyer?"

"Going on eight years, not counting the years of law school and all." Zoey pauses, but Molly's intent expression indicates her interest, so she continues. "I'm in civil rather than criminal law. I've always loved the law, both criminal and civil." She stops short, takes the last bite of chocolate, and only then continues, "My mother was a doctor. She thought I'd make a good one because she said I'd have a great bedside manner. But I am not at all a blood and guts, pain person."

Molly decides to ask the question that is hovering between them, "Zoey, your mother, is she ..."

Before she can finish the question, Zoey cuts in. "My mother died. Three years ago. It was just ... there are no words to say how terrible it was. It broke my father."

Molly lets her just be.

"She was killed in a car crash."

Molly shakes her head. "I'm so sorry."

Zoey explains, "My dad just worked and worked to get through the grief. You know, I did, too. It was our way to cope with the insanity of it all." Her eyes well up, and she looks away, reaches into her purse for a tissue, but Molly has already put one in her hands. Zoey's throat has tightened, and her voice is hoarse. "Oh, God. I'm sorry. I don't talk about this to anyone."

"Zoey, we all suffer from disasters, especially when they come without any warning." Molly now understands what Alan must feel about his only child. "You are your father's pride and joy, Zoey. That is obvious."

A beat. Tears subside. Molly touches Zoey's hand. Zoey recovers. "Thank you, Molly."

Another roar comes from the theater, and this soothes both women.

Zoey, clearly wanting to change the subject, says, "And here you are, Molly, a famous actress. I bet you have stories to tell about all your time on the stage with those handsome actors."

Molly laughs, and all the tension is relieved. "So, I was in lots of ensembles in Los Angeles with revival shows like *Evita* and *West Side Story*, but I wasn't the lead. Then a director saw me in *West Side Story* and asked me to audition in New York for a play he was staging Off Broadway called *Hairspray*..."

"Oh, wow. I loved *Hairspray!*"

"...and I was cast as a dancer and understudy. When I was in *Hairspray,* I saw Meryl Streep backstage and, later, John Travolta. I worked for the next two years there in smaller productions, but nobody famous comes to Off-Off Broadway. But it was just a terrific time for me back then." After a bit of banter—Off Broadway, Off-Off Broadway and the like—Molly asks, "Have you ever seen the documentary *Twenty Feet from Stardom?*"

Zoey answers that she hasn't but has heard of it.

"Well, you should see it if you can stream it. It is very much how I feel about the acting world and how much luck and timing affect those of us who were steps away from center stage."

Their conversation comes to an abrupt end as a huge round of applause comes bursting through the doors of the theater, which Alan is hastily opening. They can see the audience standing, clapping and shouting their approval for the play.

Zoey heads to the front of the lobby and opens those doors to the cool, fresh air as the patrons pour out of the theater. Alan is smiling and shaking a few hands of those he knows, and Molly is observing just how much praise is being exchanged among the departing crowd.

It takes a full thirty minutes for the theater to empty, the crew to finish up their tasks, and for Alan to walk through the seating to pick up leftover programs and such. Molly waits patiently with Zoey so she can say goodbye to him.

"I think tonight can be labeled a success," Alan says as he walks up to the two of them. "I'm relieved."

"It sure seems so," Molly tells him. "Great crowd, great enthusiasm, terrific work by the crew, and Zoey and I managed to collect a King's ransom." She laughs. "I have to get going now, but I wanted to tell you," she touches Zoey's arm and looks toward Alan, "just how much I enjoyed meeting you both."

Zoey gives Molly a side hug, "Molly, it was great talking with you. Dad, you didn't get to spend much time with her, so let's make sure we see her soon, okay?"

Alan shakes Molly's hand and affirms, "Absolutely. Just not when I am under the gun with this theater job. Can we walk you to your car?"

"Oh, well. Sure. I parked a couple of blocks away. That would be nice. I live in Little Italy for now, and I am still getting my bearings."

Zoey puts Molly between her and her father, and the three head south down Main Street. "I love Little Italy," Alan says. "When I was in court, I'd sometimes walk over there for lunch. Here, if you don't mind, put your number in my cell phone. Maybe we can meet. I'll text you."

Molly adds her number to Alan's contacts and then hands Alan her phone. "Alan, if *you* don't mind, can you put your number in mine, too? I think my sister is planning a birthday party for us, and I'd love for you guys to come."

Alan obliges and returns Molly's phone to her. "Oh," she says, "here's my car. Zoey and Alan, it was a pleasure meeting you."

Molly barely has time to start up her car when her phone sends a notification. It's a text from Zoey: *My Dad's already asking about you.*

# Act 3:
# The Revival

## Act 3, Scene 1:
# Of Teachers, Lawyers, and Actresses

"Blow out the candles before you two set off the smoke alarm!"

Callie and Molly each inhale and then exhale, blowing out the many, many candles on their birthday cake. Hello, age 60! The twins cheer and applaud right along with all their friends at Carlo and Carmen's Italian bistro.

Alan Bernstein stands in the outer ring of guests surrounding the sisters. He was surprised to be invited, being such a recent acquaintance of the O'Toole twins, but here he is. He's alone because his usual date, Zoey, has a date tonight herself. With a teacher named Dan. Alan told her he approves.

Patrick and Renee insisted he come to the party for reasons that Alan assumes have something to do with the theater. Tom also urged him to come, using as the excuse that the party would need more men to mingle with the twins' women friends. So, here he is.

Alan had staked his reputation as a lawyer on his ability to listen. His mentors had told him there was nothing to be gained by talking *over* someone or talking *at* someone. The most valuable evidence needed to establish the truth, he learned, was offered by those who either intentionally or accidentally just could not stop talking.

So, this evening, he watches and listens. He's feeling awkward. Most of the people around him are Callie's former teaching colleagues. As often as Tom comes by to refill his Chianti, and as often as Carlo reminds him of all the good times he has shared in their bistro, he can't quite relax. *Sophie is not here.*

Sophie would be nudging him to loosen up and offer a toast to the good times being shared. He would be holding her hand. He would be getting her a slice of cake. He would be dancing with her when the music called them.

This is the first party he's attended since Sophie's death. There might have been some sort of celebration when he retired, but he hadn't been up to it. He'd just disappeared.

He smiles at the fading candle's glow. The thing to do is to stand still, smile, laugh when appropriate, and listen. He doesn't know Callie very well. Though there were occasions when he and Sophie had dined with the Kents, he and Tom spent most of dinner talking about basketball or politics while Sophie and Callie chatted about books, movies, their careers and, occasionally, their stubborn husbands.

The teachers congregate around Callie. One mentions how inspired she was when she began her career by having someone like Callie to turn to when students didn't listen or didn't seem reachable. The others talk about their own retirement plans—travels to Italy, France, or national parks.

Traveling. An oppressive shadow slides across Alan's mind. He's eavesdropping on adventures he had planned with Sophie. Romantic. Mysterious.

He'd told his psychologist that his grief showed itself to him as a shadow always lurking on the fringes of his mind. The darkness passed through the walls of his kitchen each time he forced himself to eat, alone. It was waiting for him on business trips in every empty hotel room with a phone by a bed he could never again use to call her at home, hear her voice.

Then, he'd never felt alone, even when he was away. Despite the distance, they always had a nightly phone call, and they would always say *I love you.*

He does not wish to be invited to his former colleagues' parties. He knows that the invitations he's received have an unspoken purpose—to help him adjust to being without a companion, a job, a confidant ... a lover. To adjust to a new companion, perhaps, a similarly alone and lonely woman they've invited. No, *no thank you.* It would feel like a pity party.

It's nobody's fault, really. And that's why Alan Bernstein remains so angry. There is no one to sue, to take to court. There is no fault. A lawyer wants to know that there is fault, and that events do not lie in the stars but with the cold, hard facts of life. There should be justice.

He does not want to continue to live like this. He assumed that three years of sessions with his doctors and depression meds would rescue him. But he's beginning to realize that there is no expiration date for love. When it is lost, it is never forgotten. His therapist told him he's been through the six stages of grief, but the seventh one—acceptance—takes its own time. "The first time you can actually laugh about a memory of Sophie ... really laugh ... that's when you will be on your way to healing."

Alan is still waiting for that laugh.

Why is it, he wonders, that every moment full of light for everyone around me is, for me, so dark?

So here Alan stands with his hands in his pockets holding a position against the darkness.

And just then, Molly O'Toole appears before him with two plates holding slices of her birthday cake. "You look like a man who could do with a delicious piece of chocolate cake."

He shakes his head, waking from his trance.

"Are you feeling all right, Alan?"

"Oh. Yes. Sorry. I was just thinking ..."

Molly smiles, "You sound like Walter Mitty."

"Sorry I'm distracted." He smiles back at her. "Of course, I'd love a slice of your birthday cake, and I must congratulate you on another successful trip around the sun."

"Thank you. I'm not sure it was *successful*, though. Let's just say that I feel I have at least landed on my feet." Molly tilts her head toward the far end of the restaurant toward an empty table. "Speaking of which, I'd love to get off my feet. I've been standing for too long, chatting away. Let's go sit." Warmth radiates from her eyes. *She may be a bit tipsy.*

"Good idea. You take the plates. I'll get us coffee."

"Oh, good. With a splash of milk, please, Alan. I probably need to sober up a bit." A laugh bubbles up.

He's happy to have a purpose. Coffee. Cream. Napkins. He turns and sees Molly at the table. *Ready, march.*

They sit and sip and sigh.

Molly breaks the silence. "Alan, I wanted to ask you ... wait, I think that you and I are maybe the only two people here who are not teachers."

"Yes. I noticed. I can see how much your sister matters to her colleagues."

"I invited some of my L.A. friends, but you know actors. Always busy."

"Actually, you are the only actress I have had the pleasure to meet."

"Well, trust me. Actors tend to be flighty, like hummingbirds, you know. They are all around and you can hear them flitting from flower to flower, but it's damn hard to see them stop even for a second. I guess that was me, too."

Alan nods, "Lawyers can be very much the same. Always running from court to court, always a witness to question or a brief to file. I guess that was me, too."

They both smile. Alan follows up, "So what do you want to ask me?"

Molly leans in, "Right. Well, besides the fact that I'd like to know more about you other than that you've raised a lovely daughter, I feel a little ambushed tonight."

"Oh, so you didn't know about the party?"

"No. I did." She takes the tiniest sliver of cake on her fork and tastes it. "The ambush came from my old pal Patrick."

"Really?" Alan takes a bite of cake as well.

"Yep. He cornered me and pitched me this *grand* idea. Long story short, I know that COVID really wiped out their theater for over a year, and Renee has told me that they're slowly crawling back money-wise. But ... Patrick asked me to be involved in a fundraiser."

Alan's eyebrows lift. "Oh, well, is that an ambush?"

She points her fork at him. "Good point. *Ambush* is too devious a word. He knows that I've told Renee I'm done with acting, but he wants me to do a one-night fundraiser—a play—it's called *Love Letters*. It's about two lovers reading the letters they have written to each other over the decades. This type of presentation has been done in many other cities as a way to raise funds. He told me there's an actor he knows at the Old Globe Theater in San Diego who could play opposite me."

Alan leans in, "And you told him what?"

Molly sips her coffee. "I told him that, one, it's my birthday, so give me a break. Two, I don't want to go backward in my life. Three, he's crazy to think that I was some kind of *draw*. As if *Molly O'Toole's* name on a marquee could convince patrons to dig down into their supposedly deep pockets."

Alan listens, as is his habit, and then launches into a rebuttal. "You are likely wrong about two of your points. Yes, a birthday party is not the time, I grant you. I also want to add that I am not involved in any way in this *ambush*. As for going backward in life, I'll leave that alone. But Zoey called my attention to your career, and I spent a bit of time ... Molly, you are a very accomplished actress."

Molly ducks her head slightly. She's modest about her reputation. But she's smiling and looks surprised that Alan has taken the time to look at her old movie clips.

"Zoey shared some videos of you in several plays. You have a lovely voice and a presence on stage that ... oh, I'm just going on too much. This is very unlike me. So I'll just put it simply: I think you are an extraordinary actress. Okay?"

He swallows the last of his coffee. Half his cake is still on his plate.

Molly shakes her head. "Oh, Alan. You are being very nice, but I'm sure those credits were decades ago, and besides, I just don't want to fall back into my old ways."

She finishes her coffee. She has left half of her cake on her plate.

A beat.

Alan continues, "I'm sure you don't have to decide tonight."

"You're right. I'm not sure how to handle this. I don't want to come across as a diva who doesn't want to be bothered to help, but by the same token, I only vaguely know the play he's referring to and, well ... if I did it, and that's a big if, it would be a one-time thing. As a favor to an old friend. Once and only once."

Alan nods, then asks, "Do you want my opinion?"

"Yes. Yes."

This time, it is Alan who shakes his head. "You hardly know me, Molly. What if I say you should never have given up acting? You are too good. Too talented."

Molly stops him. "Alan, stop. Let me tell you one thing I have already figured out about you, okay? You are a listener."

"Well, thanks, but ..."

Molly continues, "I've been watching you, tonight and at the play. I saw how you observed people. You strike me as other-centered. I gathered that from Zoey when she and I talked. You worry about her more than yourself, as a good father should. So you see, I think you have *heard* me, and you know it's time for me to move on. I don't think that you'd ever try to delude me into following my lost Hollywood star."

Alan grins. "Okay. Fair enough. Here's what I think. They really could use you as a boost here at La Paloma. You are more than a local star, and you can't turn down an opportunity to help folks provide this community with the joy that comes from live performances in the theater." *He again gauges her reaction as appreciative.* "I know you said one and done, and that you'll stick to it and not retreat. I'm quite certain that Patrick and Renee would never break your trust. I'll make sure Patrick understands the conditions you set."

"As my counselor, Counselor?"

"Yes. Molly, you will be my only client." He reaches out to shake her hand.

"Well, Mr. Alan ..."

"Bernstein."

"A handshake will do. We have a deal ."

"We do."

They both look back at a party that is now winding down. Alan turns back and asks, "What did you say the play was called?"

"Love Letters."

## Act 3, Scene 2:
# A Sunset Stroll on Moonlight Beach

At low tide on Moonlight Beach in October, the water recedes so far and the sand flattens so perfectly that Molly and Renee can meander northward toward the next beach in the neighboring town of Leucadia. The Pacific Ocean is calm. When the women look west across its blue expanse toward the setting sun, they spy dolphins playing in the far-off waves on their yearly journey south to Mexico and warmer waters.

Molly asked Renee to stroll the beach with her after spending several days weighing the pros and cons of costarring in *Love Letters*. Even after talking with Alan about appearing in the play, she is still having misgivings about going back to an old, tired lifestyle. Renee is sensible. She might be able to help sort things out.

"Look! I can see at least six in their pod." Renee points, and the two squint to follow dolphin frolics. "There's no waves tonight, but when the waves are just right, they love to surf them."

"Really?"

"Yes! I've seen them pop up in a curl right next to a surfer. They usually surprise the heck out of the surfer." Renee chuckles.

"Wow. That's amazing." Molly stops to take in the descent of the sun. The clouds are transitioning slowly from white to a pastel purple. "Gosh. It's just a gorgeous sky."

"I know. Maybe if we're really lucky, we'll see a green flash."

"Ah, the green flash. I remember seeing one back when I was a teenager, taking a walk with my dad. Just as the sun is about to disappear, the combination of blue water and yellow sky creates the green. Dad said it was just like mixing paint colors. He'd only seen it once before. Well, let's hope we see it tonight.

Renee brushes her hair back. "I love autumn. The tourists are less ubiquitous."

"*Ubiquitous!* That's a pretty fancy word."

"I know. Sorry. I don't mean to sound like a professor." Renee smiles. "But I'm a voracious reader."

"*Voracious!* Listen to you, girl."

"Shuddup," Renee giggles. "Sometimes words just stick in my mind. My parents were very into education, and I thought maybe I would be a teacher, but I was a little too wild and a lot too obsessed with pop culture to want to settle into teaching."

"I'm sure you would have been a wonderful teacher. You have a way about you. You care and you're determined. Look at how you've built up your business."

"Yeah, but then I'm not the stereotype of a hairdresser, huh?"

"*Stereotypes*, ha! Actresses are stereotyped, especially if they're blonde."

Renee picks up a perfect seashell and pockets it. "Well, I'm not a person who sees a client and makes a quick judgment, especially in a town as diverse as ours. You are the exception to my rule. I liked you from the get-go. You know, my ladies who work at the shop are really interesting. A couple are actually college grads, but they chose to get into a profession that is more laid-back and hands-on. They told me stories about how manipulative and hostile the corporate world treated them. The grind some jobs demanded was just too much, and then they had children, and that changed everything. My shop allows them some flexibility. Some of the other stylists are actually artists or studying art. I suppose everyone has to follow their own spirit."

Molly takes Renee's arm, "Renee, they look up to you. I could see that both times I was at your salon. They love working for you."

Renee puts Molly's hand in hers as they walk. "Thank you. My ladies and I have formed a sisterhood. It's rare in my industry, where stylists are very transient. I pay well, and I provide benefits for them when they're with me for two years. So, they're loyal to me, and I'm loyal to them. I guess that's also rare nowadays, huh?"

They walk past a couple with an adorable border collie, which bounds over to them and licks their hands. "I would love to have a dog someday," Molly says. "I grew up with several. My father was always a dog guy."

"Oh, when we went to the reunion, I think I heard Callie mention that your dad is still with you ... in a senior facility."

"Yep. He's a character. He loves to entertain people and often plays card games with some of the patients who are struggling. He usually lets them win. He kids around with the nurses. But he is failing badly ... his mind and his body." Molly waves goodbye to the couple and their dog. The sun has now dropped below the clouds and hovers above the blue ocean. The sky begins to turn from pink to red with a yellow fringe closer to the sun.

"I'm so sorry. I know that's very hard. Both my parents passed a few years before COVID. Then the pandemic's aftereffects came. It was so difficult for Patrick and me. Well, of course, the whole world. Gosh, what am I saying?"

"I know what you mean."

"At the salon, we actually dragged a couple of chairs out the front door and cut hair outside. And the theater, oh God, we had to close it. It was a nightmare making ends meet. But here we are now, on the beach watching the sunset."

"Well, speaking of your theater, that's what I wanted to talk to you about, Renee. I thought it would be easier to talk with *you* than with Patrick about what he's asking me to do. Get my feelings out. You know about it, right?"

"Yes, we discussed it."

They turn south, back toward Moonlight Beach. Both are quiet for a few moments. Renee realizes that whatever is on Molly's mind has been troubling her since her birthday party a week ago.

As the quiet stretches into minutes, Renee decides to prompt her new friend. "Hey, just tell me what's bothering you. I won't push Patrick's plan off on you. I support his ideas, but this is totally *his* project. So, what's up?"

For the next few minutes, Renee proves that she's as good a listener as Alan is.

When there is silence again, she gestures to a rock outcropping, and they both sit. "Are you afraid of stepping back into acting?" she asks.

"Yes. If I'm being honest, yes."

"Why?"

"Because it's so intoxicating. Getting a part has been like getting high. Too high. And then, when the show's over, when the lights go down, I panic. I think I'll never get another part, that I'm not a good enough actress to get another part." Molly turns from confessing to the ocean to facing Renee. "But that's only *one* concern."

"Okay. Go on." Renee has worked with actors before and heard this. But she knows Molly has the courage to step out on a limb, or else how could she have left Hollywood in the first place?

"The other concern I have is that ... well, it's that ... this play *Love Letters* has me playing a woman, Melissa, who is the embodiment of what I dread."

Renee listens intently.

"This character, Melissa, starts out like most women ... like a girl actually, interested in boys, flirting, dating, relationships. She finds it impossible to balance her work life with her ambition to marry and have children. This is a dilemma for any young woman, but Melissa is fragile. She has no one to reveal her feelings to except her lifelong friend, Andy. She writes letters to Andy, but she dates other men and marries one of them. She finally discovers the true cause of all her dysfunction. The man she's written love letters to for decades is the man she truly loved ... but she pushed him away for reasons she can't explain, even to herself. From that point on, she can't make any decisions she can live with, and life becomes one disaster after another. So, Andy, 'the one who got away,' becomes the one she finally seduces. Eventually, after they have an affair, Andy spurns her, and her depression consumes her."

"Okay, I'm following you," Renee interjects sympathetically.

"See, Renee, her dependence on a man is so central to her happiness that without a man, she is crushed, emotionally." Molly lets out a breath.

Renee allows Molly to compose herself before she responds. "You worry that *you* are this woman? That your happiness has shifted from struggling with your acting career to becoming obsessed with finding a man?"

Molly hesitates. "Well, being so dependent on a man that I would allow myself to be controlled by him. Being dependent on a man to make me happy. That's what I'm afraid of."

Renee waits to see if Molly has more to say before offering, "Or are you worried about becoming fixated on whatever is *external* in this world when you know, deep down, that external things can't bring you joy ... or peace of mind?"

Those words expose the old scar.

Molly is trying so hard to remain in control of her emotions. And then suddenly she is feeling her fear instead of discussing why it exists. Tears well up and run down her cheeks. She gasps for air as Renee, in an effort to do something, anything, to help, removes her shawl and wraps it around her friend.

Renee realizes this upheaval has been a long time coming. Molly O'Toole is a 60-year-old woman who has escaped from her past, her craft, her men, her dream of fame, and her familiarity with time and place, all in an effort to find a place where she can be content. She can't imagine how much effort it has taken for her to keep herself on an even keel despite all the waves that have buffeted her.

"Molly, listen to me. Nothing out here. The ocean. The theater. The men. The women. Your body. Your friends. Nothing outside of you will ever make you feel at peace until *you are satisfied with your own self, your own soul.* Trust me. I was where you are years ago, with dreams that I would measure myself against. I was obsessed with what people thought of me. That's poison. Other people have their own prejudices and their own agendas. They don't exist to make you feel you're good enough. They couldn't make you okay even if they tried. As long as you lean on others to give you self-worth, you will always be ... what's the right word?"

"A fool."

"No, not a fool. You are nobody's fool! You've done things that few have the guts to do, and I'm not talking about Broadway. I'm talking about *this choice*—to go it alone. To step away from what has not satisfied you and to search for what fulfills you. What makes you feel whole? What makes you smile? What adventures do you want to experience? These decisions are now totally in your hands."

They sit for a time without words. The sun begins its dive into the horizon.

"I guess it's twilight," Molly murmurs. She turns to face Renee, "I love that you said all that to me. You knew I needed to hear it."

The sun takes a final bow into the ocean's blue waters, followed by a magic that is rarely seen in an October sky.

A green flash.

## Act 3, Scene 3:
# Liam's Love Letters

Molly wakes up from a frustrating night and not enough sleep. Despite her opening up to Renee at the beach and her newfound alliance with Alan, she still cannot decide whether to play the part of Melissa in A.R. Gurney's play *Love Letters*.

During her restless night, she had a dream about her father's and mother's love letters, which she and Callie discovered when they moved Liam to the senior care center years ago. Each told a far different story that those in the play. Mary and Liam wrote of longing and the distance that Liam's military service required. They wrote of their continued desire for each other despite all the hard times. They wrote of their dreams deferred and realized, of sights they saw that year and memories they shared through the decades. Some were funny, some were touching, some were even apologetic. They were soulmates.

She's reread the play's letters three times in the last three days. These people were so diametrically different from her mother and father. They were privileged, spoiled, and dishonest with each other. At the end of the play, they were forced to realize these terrible mistakes, and both paid a price. Melissa far more than Andy. She would be embodying a character who is diminished to the point of accepting defeat.

These are characteristics that she abhors, but she knows they're part of the human condition. Trying to play the role of Melissa requires her to feel emotions that are part of the business of any actress. But now, for the first time in her life, that business feels like poison. She can do it, once, for a good cause. But returning to her old habit, playing someone else, as actresses do, is a skin that she will shed. Underneath it, she knows she must discover the real Molly O'Toole.

Last night, when she woke up in a sweat, she told herself that this commitment would not be a revival. It would be one night only. Nor would it be about her. Friendship is what it would be about. Giving back. Raising money for a cause that has been her inspiration over a lifetime.

She texts Patrick to meet her later this afternoon after she and Callie see their father.

Today is Liam's 79th birthday. Molly prays that her father is lucid enough to enjoy the day. It will be a simple celebration with cupcakes and coffee at lunch. Nobody will sing. If they did, she can just imagine her father, loud enough to be heard over the conversation of the entire nursing home staff and residents. "Good Lord, no happy birthday stuff. I hate it!"

Last week, the sisters did a little shopping and found an Irish tweed cap, naturally in shades of green with Ireland's flag on the hat's peak. It was the only gift they knew he would enjoy unwrapping because he just did not like that center-of-attention feeling. Besides, he used to have such a cap years ago, but it had disappeared.

Molly meets up with Callie outside the facility, and the two slip into the dining room. Liam is there in a wheelchair with his day nurse and another staff member, and a few other patients are at the other tables.

"Dad!" Callie says as she quickly hugs him, "You look great."

"Yes, you do, Dad," Molly says, squeezing his shoulders and kissing him on the cheek.

Liam acts as if what's all the fuss, but his smile betrays him.

Callie faces him and says, "Daddy, you must know what today is because you are wearing your Guinness socks!" All four women chuckle at the black and gold socks that represent the beer that has always been Liam's favorite.

"Oh, yeah, these are still my favorite socks. Always have been."

"Well, it's also your birthday!" Callie proclaims.

Liam can't hide his confusion. "My what?"

Molly repeats, "Today is your 79th birthday, Dad!"

"Oh, it is? Gosh, that's good ... great. Okay. Girls, now, don't make a big fuss over me. Christ Almighty, I'm 79, huh? Okay, that makes your mother 77." He seems to drift away for a moment, maybe trying to grasp all the time that has passed.

Attendants come to the table with a tray holding a dozen cupcakes. Several other patients are wheeled in, but they seem oblivious to Liam, his daughters, and even to the cupcakes. Liam sees the tray and says, "Well, these sweets must be for me, I guess. Thanks so much, girls, and everyone, huh. How old am I? I feel like I'm 100." Everyone laughs.

Callie tips his face toward her. "Next year is the big one. 80!"

"Oh, yeah. Huh. Right. If I make it." *Nervous laughter.*

Liam slowly reaches for a cupcake, and the sisters encourage others to select one as well. "Oh, this one is very good." Liam's hands shake more than Molly expected.

His doctor told the sisters last week that he now has more days on which he struggles than when he is upbeat. The doctor also told them that he falls asleep during the day more often than he did six months ago. All this makes Molly wonder if her father distinguishes between his two daughters. She doesn't want to test him.

The cupcake crumbles in his hands, and Molly saves a chunk and helps him to gobble it up. It's upsetting watching her father, once strong and charming, struggling to feed himself. She smiles, nonetheless, and wipes crumbs from the table into her hand with a paper napkin.

After a time, the sisters wheel their father back to his room where he will be more comfortable. There, they present him with his gift. He breaks into a broad grin when he sees the cap and exclaims, "You found my old cap! Gosh, girls. Wow. I love this old cap. It's the one Mary got me when we went to Ireland. Thank you, girls. Can I have a kiss after you get done taking a picture of me? Wait till the guys see this."

There is that twinkle in his eye again, though his girls can see from his suddenly slumping posture that he will nod off soon.

When he falls asleep, Callie gets him a blanket while Molly distracts herself from her melancholy by glancing about the room. The picture of Mary and Liam on their wedding day is in a silver frame next to the lamp on the nightstand. There are two small drawers in the nightstand she's never investigated. Opening the top drawer, she can see it's full of tissues, unused wipes, and old plastic utensils. In the bottom drawer, though, under a blue velvet pouch that she knows holds her father's pocket watch, which he used to wear on special occasions, she sees a rose-colored bundle tied with a blue ribbon.

Molly catches her breath. "Oh, my God! Callie, remember when Mom and Dad had their 40th Anniversary, and we couldn't find a special gift? And then we rummaged around their bedroom and came upon all those anniversary cards Mom had saved. Then we found Dad's letters to her when he was in the Navy. Remember?"

"Oh. I think so. Oh, wait. Yes. I remember you sitting on the floor by their bed reading his letters, and you started bawling and saying that he was so romantic, even though he never acted that way in front of us. Right! I remember."

Molly reaches for the package tied with ribbon, "We gave them those letters on their anniversary that year, wrapped with a ribbon. I think I just found them!"

"Well, I was sure we kept them."

Molly brings the bundle of letters close to her face to read what is written on one of the envelopes. When she does, she breathes in the faintest scent of her mother's perfume. Or at least, she imagines the scent. She slides the bundle into her purse and kisses her father goodbye.

Later, she will be sitting on her bed reading, in tears once again.

## Act 3, Scene 4:
# Two Cups of Cold Coffee

It begins with a meeting with Patrick. Patrick tells Molly he totally understands her concerns and her position that this is a "one and done" performance. He appreciates her desire to help him and Renee with their passion project, especially since theater was her world for decades.

Molly walks out of the theater and into the bright sunshine pondering her next move. She sits in her car. She stares at her phone. She scrolls to the letter A and makes a call.

"Hello, Alan?" Her breath catches, and then she gulps a morsel of air. "It's Molly O'Toole." She knows his response will dictate her next move. She hears an energy-infused reply, "Oh, Molly, I'm so glad you called." She can settle.

She rushes through a summary of the discussion with Patrick before she comes to the ask: "Can we meet soon? I have something I want to ask you. I have two copies of the play, and I'm wondering if ... well, if you would help me prepare by running lines with me." She's so nervous she can hardly hear Alan's reply, but it does include "yes" and "great" and "the Better Buzz."

"Oh," she takes a quick breath. "That's just down the street. Yes, thirty minutes. See you then." She puts her phone down on the console and rubs the palms of her hands against her jeans. *Whew.*

The Better Buzz is the latest coffee shop to open in this beach town. Since it's past the morning rush, it's not as packed as mornings can be. Long tables on one side of the shop are where many patrons sit, and, as Molly assumes, work remotely. On the other side, there are tables for two, which is where she sees Alan. He stands to greet her, touches her forearm and asks what she would like to drink. Then, he heads to the coffee station, orders, stirs, and delivers two piping hot cups of coffee.

"So, Molly, I do know what 'running lines' means. I see actors doing that, memorizing their parts. But why do that when this play you're doing is a *reading*?"

Molly smiles. "Well, technically it's a reading, but the reality is that I have to memorize much of the part, anyway, for two reasons. First, the banter is so quick, as you will notice right away, that if I don't know what comes next, it will go too slowly. Or I'll never get to lift my head and look at my audience. More importantly, though, I really need to internalize Melissa's emotions to play her as she needs to be played."

"Ah. I get it." He asks about her coffee, and then he confesses. "Actually, I've just used an old lawyer's trick. Ask questions you already know the answer to. I watched a few clips of the play online, and what I saw was eyes up and really quick back and forth. Sorry for asking. I guess I just wasn't sure how to start our conversation."

"Oh, that's all right. I'm glad you asked. I mean, I get it, too. We've just met. Kinda awkward when we don't really know each other, huh?" A beat. "This is *really* good coffee."

"I think so. So, how are you getting along since you moved down here? Do you like Little Italy?"

"It's charming. I've met quite a few people. I love the old Italian men I see playing bocce ball several times a week when I'm out walking. Gia, my tour guide when I first moved in, she and I had lunch together. After the holidays, I'll get serious about looking for a more-than-temporary place to live here."

She waits for the typical advice from a man who thinks that he knows what she should do. It does not come. *He's just listening to me. Nice.*

"And things are good with Patrick? I don't need to threaten him with a lawsuit?" Alan grins.

"No. No. I suspect you and Renee probably warned him about my trepidations."

"Oh, no. Not me. Renee, maybe. But even if she didn't, I think Patrick's smart enough to not take advantage of a gift."

"Right." She sips. Longer pause. "So, what do you do with yourself? Uh, that came out wrong." *Nervous laugh.* "I mean, how are *you* handling retirement? Zoey told me you are newly minted. Do you miss the courtroom challenges?" *Get him to talk.*

"I don't miss the stress. Or the hours. That's for sure. Television shows make lawyering all seem so ... theatrical. I hope that didn't offend you."

*He's thinking about my feelings. Nice again.* "No offense taken. Zoey says you were a commanding presence at trial."

"She's biased. The truth is that my late wife, Sophie—she was the force of the family." He stops abruptly.

Molly divulges what she knows. "Zoey told me about her passing. I'm so sorry for your loss." *Now what do I say?* "I can't really relate. I suppose you can surmise that an actor's lifestyle makes a marriage, or in my case staying in one, a dubious choice ... at least it was for me."

"Oh. Well, Zoey and I helped each other through Sophie's death." Alan pauses for a beat. Then he acknowledges, "Molly, it's my experience that many professions make sustaining a marriage difficult. I assume your marriage faltered some time ago?"

"Yes. It was decades ago. My ex-husband was like me then. Ambitious. He was always hustling for the next opportunity. And, naturally, he wanted me with him."

"Understandable."

"And me, well, I needed to hustle, too. In my late 20s, New York was where a serious actress needed to be, as opposed to Los Angeles, where TV actors filmed."

"And you are clearly a serious actress."

"Was. Was. Past tense, Alan. Anyway, that was my dream. At least Kurt, my ex, got the fame and riches. He was on the ground floor working for a company called Pixar."

"Oh!"

"Right, and it was bought by Disney, and the rest is, as they say, history. His timing was perfect." *God, I am babbling way too much. Listen. Listen!* "Don't you agree?"

Alan slid right into the breach, "Hmm. Timing is important, but it's been my experience, Molly, that no amount of money really guarantees a happy life."

"No, it does not. He's on wife number three now, or maybe four. I lose count. Each one's younger than the one before. But to tell the truth, he's always been fair to me. We were young. Our divorce was amicable. He was generous. I'm grateful. End of story."

Alan nods. "Amicable is always the goal. I didn't always see much commendable behavior from men in divorce cases when the word got around my law office. Or from women, either, to be honest."

"I wasn't a saint, that's for sure. But that's a twisted story of two people living 3,000 miles apart. Things don't always turn out as expected." *Oh no. Why did I say that?*

"What did you expect?"

Molly does a quick course correction, "Oh, I wasn't thinking about my marriage. I was reflecting on my career. It's been 25 years by myself."

Alan's eyebrows lift. "That's a long time. I've been on my own for three years, and it feels like an eternity. Of course, it was unexpected and I'm working through ... things."

"Yes, well, expectations!" *Why do I feel I can tell him so much about myself? Should I?* "Alan, when I was an actress breaking into the business, I was often faced with ... moral decisions. For example, do I ignore my values and stay true to my marriage vows?"

"So you were married when ..."

"... when I left for New York, yes."

He grins, "You're being a bit mysterious."

"Yes. I know." And being too transparent may be the last thing I want to be.

Alan adds a teaspoon of sugar to his coffee and stirs it slowly. "Molly, you can trust me. After all, I am your lawyer."

They both laugh.

"Right, we shook on it. Okay, well, the moment of truth came to me with a wallop. I had momentum after *Hairspray*, but then the casting director for a new play implied that he could "better evaluate me"—that's how he chose to word it—if I followed him up to his hotel room."

Alan pushes his coffee away to the side of the table.

"Yeah. Well, I refused. Naturally, I lost the part even though my agent said he was sure I was a lock." *Should I go on? He hasn't once interrupted me.*

Alan clears his throat, leans forward, and whispers. "I have a bad feeling about what comes next."

Molly nods. "I called my husband later, and he chose that time to inform me he would like to have an open marriage." *Oh, God. No going back now.* "So I knew right then that I was the fool."

Alan's lips form a grimace. His eyes are intense. I feel like I'm giving testimony, but he's making no effort to lead the witness. I like that.

She continues, "I spent a while wondering if I should have slept with the sleazebag. But I didn't. The story ends with my agent telling me that this is a well-worn path for younger actresses, and that he was not surprised that I'd refused. He assured me I did the right thing. Nonetheless, the casting director ruined my reputation. From then on, I was 'difficult to work with'."

"I see. I'm sorry that it ended like that."

"After about a year of 'difficult to work with,' my New York experience was done, and I headed off to L.A. and worked in television. I was older and wiser by then. Well, that's me." *Now, what in the world does he think of me?*

Alan sits back, takes a breath, and exhales as he leans into his reaction. "I have something to tell you, Molly, "I hope you know how much I admire your tenacity and the journey you navigated to follow your dreams. I believe that the vast majority of folks are too scared to ever venture as far out there as you did. Most of us, myself included, are too cautious."

Molly starts to blurt out a reaction, then swallows it. Shut up. Let him talk. He's finally telling me about himself.

Alan fiddles with the coffee mug, then takes a sip. "I kept to the path that I was sure I could handle. I passed the bar, worked ridiculous hours, and made partner. The only ambitious act I risked was when I broke off with some of my like-minded associates and started my own firm. I'm a one-trick pony. And I had a lot of breaks go my way."

Molly then follows suit, taking a dainty sip of her now lukewarm brew. "You are being very self-effacing, Mr. Bernstein. *He really is. I like that, too.*

Alan smiles. "Since we are bearing our souls, Ms. O'Toole, the great challenge for me was our choice to have children, or in my case, a child. I was so locked into my job, as was my wife Sophie, into hers. She was just out of her residency at the time and hoping to get her medical practice started, and then having Zoey changed *everything*. God. I had to become a father. I had to rebalance my life's priorities."

I love how quietly he speaks. Measured.

"It was like swinging in this crazy trapeze act, hoping to catch your partner when she lets go in midair so we both could make it to the other side." He stops abruptly.

"You were working without a net."

"Right. And then one day, you think you have it all down to a routine."

Now he's the one hesitating to go on with the story. I wonder if he's expressed this to others. And if not, does he trust me?

"And then ... then, I couldn't catch her."

Molly realizes Alan may never recover from his high-wire act. "Oh, Alan. I am so sorry for you both."

They sit in silence, both tapping their coffee cups with their fingers and struggling to make eye contact. Molly decides that a bridge from their past lives to right now is needed. "Counselor, we have two cups of cold coffee."

"Yes, we do."

"Are you still willing to spend some time running lines with me?"

Alan smiles, "Most definitely. Just as long as nobody has the foolish idea of putting me on stage sitting opposite you."

"I promise. Patrick told me he knows an actor who'd like to get involved. Anyway, I brought a copy of the script for you." She reaches into her canvas bag and pulls out the play.

"I hoped you'd bring a copy. How about I take it with me, read the play over, and then we meet again in a couple of days?"

She nods assent. "Where would you like to meet?" *I like that he defers to me. Nice.*

## Act 3, Scene 5:
# Melissa and Andy in Love Letters

Alan decided to take the trolley down to Little Italy and walk to Molly's condo in the heart of town rather than drive down and compete with all the tourists for a parking space. *Walking will do me good.*

On the thirty-minute ride south along the coast, he has time to consider what Molly may be asking of him. *What does she think of the play?* He did not expect it to have such a tragic ending with the woman, Melissa, dying due to her prolonged dependence on alcohol and eventually her addiction to painkillers. The male character, Andy, is unable or unwilling to help her. *Hell, he is part of her addiction.*

He walks down India Street and notices new banners on the street lights featuring famous Italian-Americans like Pacino and De Niro. He and Sophie loved coming here for dinners back before the pandemic, back when his world made far more sense. He smiles when he turns on Beech Street and looks up to see Bruce Springsteen's face on the corner streetlamp. *Hmm. Didn't realize he was Italian.* He makes a left onto Columbia Street and spots Molly's condo building.

He checks the address, then checks his watch. *Right address and on time. Good.* He rings the doorbell and hears Molly's voice saying she'll be right there. *Why am I nervous?*

Molly opens the door, and the first thing he notices is her forest green turtleneck, which accentuates her green eyes. She's dressed casually in blue jeans and three-quarter high taupe desert boots. No jewelry. Little makeup. Her curly hair has been pulled back in a ponytail. *Probably easier to read that way. Hair won't get in the way.* Her smile is warm.

"Alan, please come in." She looks outside. "Gosh, it's foggy today. I'm so thankful you drove all the way down here."

"My pleasure. Actually, I took the trolley. I parked at the Veterans Hospital in La Jolla, and it was just a short trip down here, and the walk was just two blocks. Besides, I love Little Italy. It's been a while since I've been here." He follows her past the living room to the kitchen. He means to comment on the condo, but he is distracted. *She is at ease, or seems to be. And lovely.*

"Carlo and Carmen, you remember, are being so generous, letting me stay here until I'm settled. This was their first home when they came from Milan. Usually, their relatives stay when they visit the States, or they rent it out. I won't take advantage." She points to the kitchen table, where two glasses of water sit side by side, "I'm just starting to look for a small place up in your area, even though I'm starting to feel like this village is growing on me. I hear that it's better timing to wait until after the holidays."

"Carlo and Carmen were terrific hosts for your birthday celebration, and they do know how to party!" They both laugh, then chat about the weather, the local restaurants and the condo.

Molly hops up and says, "My gosh, I forgot to offer you coffee. We got to talking and I lost my head. Coffee?"

"Yes, please." She pushes a few buttons, and the coffee percolates. She pours, adds milk, and slides back into her chair next to him. "So, what do you think of the play?"

"Well, I can see why it's been popular, and it certainly fits the bill as a fundraiser because it is so easy to produce—no set, just two actors who don't have to memorize everything. Shoot, they don't even move, right?

"Right. No blocking."

"Ah, yes. That's the term. But."

"But?"

Alan continues, "But it's bittersweet. It's really a lot of things. Funny. Touching. But in the end, tragic. Melissa and Andy are mostly sad characters with regrets. Regret seems to be the play's theme."

Molly nods. "Yes. It is. Yes. You've ..."

He waits for her to continue. Something is troubling her. Let me change directions.

When she doesn't reply after a moment, he says, "I was surprised that it summarizes their lives from when they were teenagers to decades later. The flirtation in the beginning, well, really all the way through, that was what I thought added humor."

Molly shakes her head slightly. "Right. Yes. Right. I agree. It's charming in the beginning, at first, during Act One. And I like both the characters, and I'm pulling for them to be happy."

"Exactly."

"But ..."

"But they never really followed their heart," Alan concludes.

"Until it is too late," Molly sighs.

Until it is too late.

Alan allows the silence between the two of them to speak to the sorrow that has befallen the play's characters, but it also seems to affect Molly. They sip their coffee.

Just when the silence is about to get uncomfortable, Molly reaches into her bag and pulls out the script. "Well, do you think we should run through some of the opening scenes? That's the joyful part."

Alan follows suit, smiling. He turns to the first page but then hesitates. "Before we start, I have a question. Why didn't Melissa ever tell Andy how much she loved him when they were younger? I mean, she had every opportunity, you know? He invited her to his school, and it was obvious she really liked him, so why did she put him off?"

Molly turns to him. "Well, that's the million-dollar question. First, I should say that Andy is really kind of a nerd with all the letter writing. I mean, that's not how you get close to someone."

Alan nods. "True. That's another point I want to make. But first, tell me about Melissa."

"Okay. Here's my take. Remember, the play takes place in 1937. Women then were not what women are now. Melissa was so dependent on a man for her happiness. She, like so many women then, well, and some now, too, were destroyed by male dominance and control. Andy's obsession with the letter-writing bullshit keeps her at bay, and she lets his need for control dictate her life. Remember, they were both born rich, so when their social circles pushed them apart, they unhappily married others. Melissa never gets over the love she lets slip away."

"Yes, I agree. But then they have an affair...."

"All too late, and by then she is wounded so badly that when he cuts it off and retreats back to his wife and his secure world, which is Andy's big problem, that's the dagger to her heart." Molly points to the table with her finger to punctuate Melissa's fate.

Alan leans back. "Andy's unwillingness to communicate face-to-face is the reason that the play is titled "Love Letters." Ironic, isn't it?"

"That's the verdict I came to, Counselor. In the beginning, they were too young, but later, they were unwilling to open themselves up to each other."

Alan smiles.

Molly asks, "Why the smile?"

Alan explains, "It's sad. But I'm smiling because ... because, here we are 80 years later, and people are still doing the same thing. Okay, people aren't writing letters to each other, but they are texting, emailing. Heck, they aren't even meeting each other. They're on dating sites. My daughter has been telling me about how frustrating all that is. She tells me people lie about who they are. It's nuts."

"It's a different world, Alan."

"Yes. But I have to tell you, I think Zoey has finally met a good guy. His name is Dan. She told me he's a teacher. They met at a fundraiser for high school kids thinking about going into the legal profession. They seem to have hit it off. I've met him on a few occasions, and he seems like he has it together, unlike some of the other men she's dated. *I am getting way off track.*

It's Molly's turn to smile. "I am so happy for Zoey. Good for her ... and you."

"I sound like a grumpy old man." *I hope she doesn't think that of me. I do sound like it, though.*

"No. You're a father thinking about your daughter. Alan, I don't know you all that well, but you don't strike me as a grumpy man."

Alan looks relieved. "Thank you for that. I try to be positive and accept change. Especially since change has been thrust on me." *Should I tell her?*

"Yes, says the woman starting life all over in my second act." Molly puts her hand on Alan's. "Let's try to read the first part of the play and see how it goes, okay?"

"Okay. I'll try not to mess it up." Oh, God. I can't believe I am doing this.

"Alan. You crack me up."

## Act 3, Scene 6:
# Teddy

Twenty minutes later ...

Molly comes to an abrupt stop in her Act One monologue and turns away from the script. Alan can see that something has upset her. She excuses herself, stands, and reaches over to the kitchen counter where a tissue box lies in waiting. She takes a tissue, dabs her eyes, and then returns to the table with the box in hand.

Alan lets her settle back into her chair. He says nothing. Molly apologizes, "So sorry, Alan."

"Was I so terrible that I brought you to tears?" he asks, attempting to lighten the mood.

"No. No. No! Molly's response is a mixture of nervous laughter and declarative insistence. "You're doing great, Alan. It's me being ridiculously emotional."

He waits. Let her explain.

"It's something I pushed out of my mind because of what I did and how it ended. I haven't thought about it for decades. It just came over me. Oh Jesus, I am so embarrassed."

He waits.

She dabs her eyes and takes a breath.

Finally, he says, "We don't have to keep going."

"No. No. I'm better." But then she stands up again and this time asks him, "Alan, do you mind if we just sit in the living room for a couple of minutes? I just need to tell you something, okay?" She moves into the living room and sits on one side of the sofa. Alan sits on the opposite side.

"I guess I'm never gonna get through this play unless I let it out. I've bottled this up for so long that ... well, when you said this is a play about regrets, um ... that's what made me remember that ... I've only told one person, ever. My sister. Wait. That's not totally true. My college friends knew. Anyway ..."

Alan nods. I want her to tell me.

Molly takes a breath. "Alan, when we were reading the young love scenes of the play, I had trouble focusing because I kept being ... invaded—that's the only word I can think of—by what happened to me when I was just out of college, in 1991 or so. I think I was 24 years old, maybe. It's when I met Teddy."

Alan watches her carefully. Her tissue is balled up in her hands, which are now balled into fists in her lap.

"I was in a play with him in L.A., Teddy. We started flirting because the play, *Plaza Suite*, was one that required us to be backstage for hours waiting for our small part. So one thing led to another, and Teddy and I found ourselves making out back there ... all the time. We were being pretty risque behind the stage, and since we didn't come out until the very end of the play, we ... well, we got carried away sometimes. You get what I'm saying, right?" She gives him a look, putting an exclamation point on her message.

"I'm following."

"I was pretty naive then. God, I was just out of college and definitely inexperienced sexually, but Teddy was very attractive, and I just lost my head. I thought I was in love ... and as time went on, well, I was. None of this is exactly where I'm going with this, except that one thing led to another, and after the last performance of a four-week run, he tells me that we should get married. Mind you, he doesn't propose. He just says let's just elope ... right then. I mean, the truth was I really didn't know him all that well, but we were young, both of us actors. We were both ambitious. He was totally gregarious and very much a person who demanded control and wanted attention. And I was so, hmm, *infatuated* with him, and I loved having a man like him in my life.... I didn't even tell my parents. I just told Callie about him.

"We went to a 'marriage celebrant' guy, a very woo-woo L.A. thing to do then. I should have known that he wasn't legit when he told us that we didn't need a marriage license for him to marry us. Teddy said we could get a license later. That should have been a clue that this was bogus. Anyway, he pronounced us man and wife, and that was that." She stops and looks at Alan. "I know. Really stupid, right?"

Alan weighs in, "We all did," he pauses, "crazy things when we were young, Molly. Myself included."

"Yeah, well, I think I topped the charts. Okay, but all this is a long way from getting to the literal punch line."

Uh-oh.

"So, after the so-called marriage, we went to see some of my friends from theater at UCLA, and I introduced Teddy. That's when I saw two of my guy friends there look at each other with shocked faces. So, while Teddy was talking to some people, I cornered them and asked why they were being so weird about Teddy. Now, I knew that both of them were gay and ..." Molly stops.

"And they told you Teddy was, too."

"Yeah."

"I suppose they knew because one of them ..."

"Both of them."

"I see." Alan scratched his head. *Let her finish.*

"Later, I confronted Teddy and asked what the hell was going on. And that's when he admitted that they were telling the truth. That he felt he needed to create an identity of being a straight man ... even married. After all, he said, that was what gay actors were doing then. Remember, this was the 90s and all. He named a bunch of actors who were leading double lives, and then, of course, he apologized. He told me that he truly loved me ... it's just that our lives wouldn't be what I would want. I was angry and told him he used me. That he faked everything. I was trying to make him miserable, but that wasn't helping the situation. I didn't understand that he was not prepared to come out of the closet."

"Understandable." What an awful thing for both of them to face.

"So the story ends with him imploding. We never got a marriage license, and I tore up the ridiculous certificate from the woo-woo 'celebrant,' and that was that. Callie told me that it would be our secret, and I never told my ex-husband Kurt. For a short time, Teddy and I only communicated through a mutual friend."

Alan waits for the other shoe to drop.

That's how I found out he was seriously depressed. See"—she leans closer to Alan—"when I first read the play and got to the scenes when Melissa goes into a downward spiral and starts drinking and self-medicating, my mind flashed to Teddy. I pushed it away then, but just now, when I read the scene with you, I just lost it."

Alan touches her hand, trying to let her know he's still hearing her.

Molly regroups, "Teddy had serious sexual identity issues. He wrote to me that his parents, who were very religious, told him he was going to Hell, and they wanted him to 'fix himself' or something crazy like that. His sister wouldn't have anything to do with him, either. Only his gay friends understood, but then they were also not ready to come out yet, and so they told him to just do what he had to. He was a mess."

Molly takes a breath. "Alan, it was the letters that freaked me out. His letters to me and this goddamn play. Letters. Letters ... shit. I just finally ignored his letters. I shut him out. I just ... I had my own problems. I told myself that I forgave him, but that was so selfish because he really didn't do anything wrong. He was just trying to figure out how to survive. I was too young ... too selfish to know what to do to help him. I really did love him, or at least what I thought was love, then. And I let him go away ... scarred." She dabs her eyes again with the remnants of her balled-up tissue.

Alan strides back to the kitchen, grabs the box of tissues, and offers her reinforcements. But he knows she needs more than tissues. She needs time to decompress. So, he waits.

Molly thanks him and takes another long breath. Then she nods. "I tried to find out many years later, out of guilt I suppose, how he was doing, but Teddy had just disappeared. Finally, I got a phone message on my machine from one of those UCLA guys I knew. This was after I was married, and all the guy said in the message was that Teddy was in a bad way." "He said that he heard Teddy had cancer. He left a number on our machine, which I immediately wrote in my diary and erased from the machine so my husband wouldn't know anything.

I didn't do anything for a while. When I finally called the number, it was no longer in use. So I never found out what happened to him. So then ..."

"When *Love Letters* ends, and Melissa dies ..."

"Right ... Teddy."

For Alan, Molly's confession is unfamiliar territory. Sophie always took care of me ... of Zoey. Maybe it's time for me to see what a burden that is.

"Molly, listen to me. I think your regrets about Teddy are commendable, but you're not guilty of selfishly ignoring him. Look, in my marriage. My wife, Sophie, often felt it was her responsibility to take care of everything and meet all our needs. It is ... it was how she, and maybe many women, are conditioned. We talked about this, about how she often ignored her own needs. It took us a long time, and a few arguments along the way, for me to get it and for her to step back."

He squeezes her hand. "So that's a roundabout way for me to say this: Molly, you were not a therapist. You weren't financially secure at that time. You were just young, and you couldn't save him. So, please, stop blaming yourself. Okay?"

"Oh, Alan. Sophie was a very lucky woman."

"Oh, no. I was the lucky one."

## Act 3, Scene 7:
## Zoey

Zoey finds her father in the kitchen stirring red sauce with his favorite wooden spoon, which has been in the family's kitchen for years. He's wearing his Berkeley dark blue sweatshirt with GO BEARS emblazoned on the back, his usual garb on Saturdays when his Cal Bears battle in the Big Game against their archrival, Stanford. His gray hair is still moist from a morning jog and the shower that followed. His hair is slightly longer than he kept it when he was at his firm. It now brushes the top of his ears. His reading glasses are perched on top of his head, keeping the longer hair from cascading over his forehead.

Midmorning sunlight filters through the flower box side window, casting a yellowish glow over a late autumn morning. "I guess you're fired up for the Big Game, huh?" Zoey strolls into the kitchen, past its island with four high stools, and closes in on the stove to give her father a hug. She sniffs the aroma of tomato sauce with meatballs bobbing to and fro in the pan and looks up at him. "So, you're making pasta today. All for yourself? That's unusual." She raises her brown eyebrows knowingly.

"Not just for me, kiddo," he replies.

"Oh, I see. Let me guess ... Molly O'Toole just may be coming over tonight?"

"You should have been a detective rather than a lawyer."

She takes the wooden spoon from him, dabs her pinky finger in the sauce, and tastes. Then, following up on the detective line of questioning, she asks, "And you two are ...?"

"Just running lines with her for her play, Inspector." He smiles.

"I see. By the way, it needs a touch more salt."

"Okay, but just a touch. And since you are in my kitchen, if you have time to hang out for a while, you could grate some cheese, and I don't think it's too early to have a little glass of Chianti, which I conveniently opened for the sauce."

"Ah, put me to work the moment I come in, huh?" She grins, "I have time and I like wine."

"Maybe you can update me on life outside of your law firm." Alan moves to a stool, and the two sit. "For example, I know you and Dan—he is still a thing, I take it—have been seeing each other more?" He pulls out another wine glass, pops the cork, and pours a splash for them both. They tap their glasses. "Cheers."

With the wine poured, the parmesan grated, and the sauce stirred and reduced to a simmer, Zoey decides the time is right. "Yes, Dad. I want you to know that your curiosity is appreciated. However, there are a couple of things I'd like to ask you about."

"Shoot."

"Okay." She leans forward. "First of all, Dan and I are, as you surmised, seeing a lot of each other. I know I don't tell you much ..."

"And I rarely ask. That was your mother's department."

"Right. Well, Dan asked me if I would like to head north this Christmas to do a little skiing, but primarily to see his parents in Sacramento. What do you think?" She reaches for her wine to gauge the impact of this announcement.

"Oh." Alan's mind races. This is unfamiliar territory again. This is the conversation mother and daughter have, which is eventually translated appropriately to me. Sophie would know exactly what to say ... she's gone, and I'm all Zoey has. "I see. Well, things are certainly moving along with you two. How long have you guys been seeing each other?"

"Well, almost a year since we first met, but we've been more serious about our relationship for the last six months."

"That's good."

"Okay, but you haven't answered my question."

Alan stops stalling. "Right. Two things I would like to know, and I hope I am not prying too much, but how do you feel about Dan? How does he feel about you? I ask because you certainly don't need my permission for, well, anything."

Zoey reaches out for her father's hand. "Dad. I am falling in love with him. He is so different from the other men I have been with. He's kind. He's so together. He's traveled. He's really smart. He loves what he does ... teaching. We have the same beliefs. And he's already told me that ... *he loves me*." Zoey looks at her father intently. "I haven't told you much because, well, I'm superstitious. I thought that any day I would find out something that would be not ... right with us. But the more I'm with him, the more I feel warm and happy."

Alan smiles and squeezes her hand, "Do you think this trip north is more than just a ski trip?

She takes a breath and, like her father, waits a moment before responding. "Maybe."

Alan glances back at the saucepan to make sure the sauce isn't overheating and to give his daughter time to respond.

"But, Dad, I'm worried that we'll be gone the entire week of Christmas, and you'll be alone. We've never been away from each other at Christmas. And Mom ..."

"Stop right there, Zoey. If this trip is what I think it may be, then I am not going to be the one to hold you back. You've got to find out how you and Dan can be together. You know what I mean? Look, I'm not good at this. Your mother had the words ... the wisdom." He stops abruptly.

Then, he sits up straighter on the stool. His posture implies that he has an oration of sorts. *Now it's time.* "Zoey, something happened to me when I was with Molly ..."

"Oh?" She looks worried.

"And it has to do with you. Molly was telling me about a regret, a serious one, she had when she was young ... younger than you are now. And when Molly and I talked just the other day, I remembered something that your mom and I had to work through many years ago."

He breathes in. "Zoey, your mom once told me that she was conditioned, like a great many women are, to take care of everyone else's needs, and many times she would either ignore her own needs or delay what she wanted for herself. My conversation with Molly reminded me of that because she once had to decide to care for someone else's needs ... but she thought that she failed that person. She's felt guilty about that ever since."

"Zoey, I want you to be aware of what *you* need right now, and if that is being with Dan, then that is what you need for yourself. For your happiness. You may be taking steps toward a serious commitment or even, like you implied, marriage. So, I need you to know that taking care of my needs is not what should drive your life's decisions. The same is going to be true when it comes to Dan's needs. Follow your heart and what you need. Asking me what I think or what Mom would have thought is okay, but ..."

Zoey reaches across the island for her father's other hand. "I know, but I have *you* now. You matter to me. I don't want you to be ..."

He cuts her off. "Alone. Forget that. I have friends. We will spend many other Christmases together." Alan lets that register and then continues, "But as your only parent, all I can ask is that I get to spend more time with you and Dan. I mean, I don't really know him very well. I like him. But if we could spend some time before you leave, then I would feel better about everything regarding Christmas. If this trip is an overture to what I suspect may be coming next, we will have special occasions to plan."

He has led Zoey in the direction he intends.

"Dad. Dan and I have been talking about marriage. About how we feel about whether or not we would want to have kids. We are in the same place in our lives, but this trip will allow us to focus away from all the distractions and just be.

Alan smiles broadly, "All right then, can we plan dinner before you leave?"

"Oh, Dad. Of course." Zoey relaxes, and she leans back as her father pours her another splash of the Chianti.

"Good. But you said you have two things to tell me."

She swirls the wine around before taking a sip. "Dad, it's about Molly and ... Mom."

He waits. He adds a splash of wine to his glass, too.

Zoey treads carefully. "I know you're spending a lot of time with Molly, and I'm glad. I really like her. But how do you feel about having a relationship with another woman?" Now she waits on him.

"Well, you assume that we are in a relationship." *Am I?*

"I suppose I am. Are you?"

Alan thinks this is a perfect time to stand up, grab his wooden spoon, and stir the sauce. He decides the temperature is a tad too high and turns the heat down. "I don't know."

"What do you think Molly feels?"

Alan returns to the island and shakes his head. "I honestly don't know that, either. We've had some compelling—the right word would be *revealing*—talks." He straightens up and squares his shoulders toward Zoey, "Right now, I feel like I very much enjoy her company. I look forward to seeing her."

Zoey understands her father's need to keep his feelings close to his chest. "That's good, Dad."

Alan counters, "Let me ask how you feel about me being in a relationship with another woman?"

She cocks her head and takes another sip. "Like you said to me, I'm not the one to hold you back."

"Touché." He looks around at the kitchen that he and Sophie remodeled after twenty years of putting up with cracked linoleum flooring and old appliances.

"Look, Zoey. Almost all of my adult life has been with your mom. She set the course for me ... for us. She plotted the longitude and latitude. So when you asked me about Dan and you leaving for the holidays, I immediately flashed to her. I would go along and defer to her because I had faith that she knew what to do. Now? Now, the onus is on me."

"No, it's not. It's on me. I'm the one responsible for me and my happiness. You and Mom have done all you can do. You always downplay your impact on me. You're the reason I'm a lawyer. You're the one who helped me to stand up for myself in a man's world. You matter so much to me, and I will always be grateful for all your love and your wisdom." She moves around the table. "I love you so much." She slides from her stool and embraces him. She buries her face into his chest. They hold this moment longer than they have for a long time.

Zoey decides to make one last point. "Dad. I am a woman. I know something about women, especially ones who have careers and are now alone ... and sometimes lonely. Molly doesn't need to rehearse her lines with you. She's a pro. She already knows her lines. Molly accepted your dinner invitation because she wants to be with you, Dad. It's obvious."

"Hmm."

"You say you've talked. Well, I know you. She's probably talked, and you've listened. Before you met Molly, you've been, damn it, what's the word? Ah, got it. *Melancholy.* But when she's with you, how do you feel?"

"I feel alive."

"Exactly. So maybe it's time to talk to her about Mom."

Alan takes a step back from her and nods. He runs his hands through his hair and knocks off his reading glasses, unaware that they've been on his head. He laughs at his own foibles. "I guess I'm a little absent-minded. Thanks for setting me straight. By the way, when did you get to be as perceptive as your mom, huh?"

## Act 3, Scene 8:
## Sophie

Molly drives into Old Encinitas and turns onto Third Street. She sees homes here that were built in the 1930s before Moonlight Beach even had a name.

The whole drive up from Little Italy, she has been pondering Alan's dinner invitation, wondering what it means. She and Alan have practiced *Love Letters* several times, and each time he has revealed only a small part of his past. *What do I know about him?* She asks herself. *"Let's see, he was a lawyer. Check. He must be in his 60s. Check. His daughter follows his lead. His wife, a doctor, died suddenly. He never mentioned any other relationship. Check, check, check.*

What it must have been like having a wonderful marriage, never experiencing the seduction, separation, and scandal. All those things I wished I had never experienced.

Molly drives past two famous boat houses built in 1929 on the southernmost part of the street. Each appears to be the bow of a large fishing boat nestled into the side of the hill. They're now a must-see tourist attraction in Encinitas.

Before there were so many tourists, way back when she was in middle school, her father had taken her and Callie there to meet the boathouse owners and take a tour. Everything seems so retro here, timeless, like her memory of two sisters trotting to the beach with that lone palm tree—which was then half the size it is now. Today, it's the symbolic lighthouse that draws people to Moonlight Beach.

She pulls into Alan's driveway. His house is from the 1940s, with clapboards and olive green and white trim and framed by two ancient ficus trees that will turn gold in the fall. Molly steps out of her car and walks to the front door, trying to ignore her fluttering heartbeat.

The door opens. Alan. "Hello, you." He smiles.

"Hello, you." She smiles. How am I supposed to greet him?

Alan pivots and motions, "Please come in, Molly." She brushes past him. "I'm sorry. I'm not much of a host. Well, I don't entertain much ... except Zoey." *He is as nervous as I am.*

"Alan, I've walked past your house—these houses—hundreds of times when Callie and I went to the beach." She gazes into his living room with its mission-style furniture, dark wood trim, and oatmeal-colored cushions and side chairs. Several seascape watercolors adorn the walls. The front bay window opens westward, and shadows seem to wash the room. "Your house is lovely."

"You're looking west," he says. Our neighbors across the street and the homes on the two streets behind them get the sunset views. We ... I ... um, get the shadows of the setting sun. Even that much sunset makes this room warmer in the summer, but the breeze keeps it comfortable. Oh, please, I'm so sorry. Let me take your coat and purse. See what I mean, not a practiced host." He laughs and gently places both on a table. "Let's wander into the kitchen. That's really my turf. Some men are into their garage. I don't have one. The kitchen is where I spend most of my time."

Molly follows him. "Smells delicious. I didn't know you were also a cook, Counselor." She smiles at him. "Actually, I don't know all that much about you except that you seem to have pretty much memorized your own lines in the play. Bravo to that."

I wonder if he notices how nervous I am.

He shows her around the kitchen, pointing out the renovations, and then the two take places at opposite ends of the kitchen island.

His chattering is off-character. He usually just cobbles a few words together and mostly listens to me. Is it because we are in his house? Is it because this is a date rather than a practical place for a rehearsal? Is it a date?

"I'm kinda behind on the holiday decorating. I actually bought a Christmas tree a few days ago. It's sitting in the backyard in a bucket of water. I need to get my act together ... so to speak."

Molly settles more comfortably onto her stool. "I don't have much in holiday decorations now that I've moved. Just one box, and I'm not sure which unopened box it is."

Alan replies, "So then, we are both in transition. Except mine is years in the making." He asks if she would like a glass of wine, and if so, white or red.

"Well, tough choice. I have a feeling red is the option that will go best with whatever you've planned for dinner."

"Good call." Alan reaches for the merlot and holds it up for her to see. She nods, and he reaches for the corkscrew, then slaps his forehead in mock horror. "No corkscrew," he says. "Damn grown children. I'll be right back." He goes to the storage cabinet out back to look for it.

Molly drifts into the living room to take in the sunlight. Sunset is turning the living room walls gold. She acknowledges the transition of color as several quiet minutes pass. She moves languidly, glancing at the photos on the sofa table. She sees a picture of Alan, presumably at his retirement, with two other well-dressed men, smiling broadly. There's also one of him and Sophie, he in a suit and she wearing her white doctor's lab coat, and another of Zoey in her law school graduation gown. She perches on the sofa.

Alan returns with a corkscrew. "Lucky I had another one stashed away," he says. He opens the merlot and pours. "Those homes across the street, those are the ones with the Sunset Magazine views. When Sophie and I moved here 25 years ago, this house had been neglected. It was a complete fixer-upper. Money was tight back then, and we had to make do and fix things as we could. That's still what I'm doing." He chuckles as he sets down the bottle and sits next to her.

Molly readjusts herself on the couch's cushion. Before Alan can launch into another monologue about the house, the neighborhood, or all the things he has not gotten to since he retired, she says, "Thank you for a lot of things, Alan."

"Oh? Well. You're welcome, but you don't have to thank me. What did I do other than just welcome you?"

Molly puts her wine glass down. "Let's see, being one of my first new friends here. For patiently listening to me the other day when I got emotional. For spending time with me on the crazy idea of doing a play. And for introducing me to Zoey. Wait, and for being my counselor, too." She takes her wine glass and tips it towards his glass. "Cheers!" *She wonders if he picks up on what she has not said.*

Alan nods, "Molly, it's been my pleasure. Are you hungry?"

"Famished."

"Then let's get this show on the road."

With the rigatoni bolognese devoured and the bottle of wine tipped so that the last drops are parsed between the two of them, Alan asks if there is anything Molly would like. "Coffee later, perhaps?"

"That would be nice. This was such a treat. Delicious. You told me you were a one-trick pony when it came to cooking. I think you've been downplaying your talents, Mister."

"Better to set the bar low than create high expectations and fall flat." He pauses. "I'm glad you enjoyed it. Much more fun to cook for two, you know."

"I'm easy to please. For far too many years, I wouldn't touch pasta because I had to keep my weight just so. This was liberating."

Quiet. They sip the last of their wine.

Alan ends the hush. "I noticed you didn't bring your script."

"No. I'm going to try going off-script. I'm sure it's not exactly necessary, and I'll probably mess things up, but you can cue me." *What I really need to see is how he speaks his lines. He's noticeably capturing Andy's character.*

"Oh, well, okay then." Alan hesitates, then grabs plates and silverware and trundles off to the kitchen. "Don't move, Molly. I'm just going to put these in the sink and grab my script. I'll deal with the dishes later."

"Oh, I don't mind helping you."

"Nope. You're the guest, and besides, we have work to do, and ..."

"And?" He acts like he wants to quit the small talk and tell me something, but every time I think he's about to go wherever he really wants to ... he just doesn't. Odd.

"And." he clears his throat and sits down on her side of the island. "I don't really know what I'm about to say because, being a lawyer, I prepare a speech for the jury. But other than with Zoey and my doctor, I haven't spoken about Sophie to anyone. So, this might come out ... raw."

She waits.

"Two things converged in my life at the same time, and I'm so grateful for both. One of them is working on this play and thinking about Melissa and Andy and all their regrets. That has had me up nights reflecting on my own life. But far, far more important is meeting you and hearing you open up to me. Trusting me with your life's highs and lows."

"Mostly lows." Don't interrupt him, Molly.

"How much courage you have to be so vulnerable to me ... a man you don't really know all that well. There's a reason you don't know me. It's because I haven't let you. I've been closed off since Sophie died. I've had no curiosity to look for ... other avenues of happiness. And I'm just too damn angry. I've been just passing time. It's like I'm punishing myself because Sophie was taken from me."

He clears his throat.

"I try to settle myself—*settle* isn't the right word, but I can't think of a better one. I think Sophie would not want me to waste my days, shut myself out. She would think me a fool."

Molly's eyes are fixed on his. No man she's known has ever spoken of heartbreak and loss so painfully. I want to cry, but no, I am not going to.

"So I want you to know how I lost Sophie." Big breath. Then another.

"Her sister lived in Rhode Island. Providence. It was April, 2020. COVID was spreading like wildfire on the East Coast. Nobody knew what it was or how it was being transmitted. You remember the panic then."

"Of course."

"Anyway, Sophie gets a call. She was a doctor, an OBGYN, she gets a call from her brother-in-law that her sister, Diana, is in critical condition in the hospital. Sophie calls me and tells me she's going to fly out there asap. I help her book a flight and ask her if she wants me to come with her, but she insists I stay with Zoey. She takes the red eye, lands in the morning, and takes a taxi to the hospital."

Molly's body tenses with each sentence Alan utters. *His voice is starting to crack.*

"The police call me. Sophie's been in a car accident. It's serious. I'm beside myself. I try to find out her condition. No word. Nobody knows anything. Two hours pass ..."

His body is shaking as if he's freezing. His teeth are chattering.

"I get a call. A doctor. He starts asking me questions about her ID. I cut him off, and I yell at him, and I ask him what is her condition. He tells me that she never made it to the emergency room."

Molly gasps.

Quiet.

Alan continues. "The car ... the car that hit her was blowing through the intersection, and the impact ... crushed her."

Quiet.

"She never regained consciousness."

Molly hears the kitchen clock ticking, but it is no match for her heartbeat. She hears Alan's breath exiting and entering through his nostrils. She dares not move.

"Before I flew out with Zoey, the police said that the other driver was having a personal emergency, and his panic is what killed him and Sophie. Only her taxi driver survived."

Alan seems lost. Molly asks, "What happened to Sophie's sister? She was in the hospital?"

Alan swallows hard. "Thankfully, she recovered, although she has experienced some bouts of long COVID. She finally told me that she feels close to 100%."

He stops to reflect. "I know Sophie's death crushed her sister's spirit. She blames herself. She regrets calling Sophie. But, of course, Sophie would have gone to her the moment she heard anything. That was just Sophie, always taking care of others ... like we were talking about the other day."

*He's exhausted. Drained.* For the first time, she reaches out to him, places her hands on his and squeezes.

Alan looks up from her hands and forces a crooked smile. The only word he can push out from his clenched teeth is ...

"Molly."

"Oh, Alan."

After a time, the emotion subsides. Alan manages a smile and says, "I know that was really hard to hear."

Molly mirrors his smile. "Yes, it was, but I'm grateful that you felt I should be aware of your loss ... and understand the circumstances."

"I didn't want to ruin your evening with my story. Actually, I hoped to end the evening with dessert—tiramisu, if you'd care for it."

Molly smiles and sits up straight. "I would love some tiramisu and an espresso. And then I'd like to know what you and Zoey are doing for Christmas."

# Act 3, Scene 9:
# Christmas Eve

Autumn has passed into winter, and the Kent dining room is set for six. Callie and Molly are in sync with preparations for their Christmas Eve dinner. The Kent's house is surrounded by Christmas lights that form white icicles, substituting for actual snow and frost, which are rare in coastal San Diego. Tom has set up his playlist of holiday songs and has champagne on ice ready.

Tom and Callie volunteered to host this post-pandemic dinner. It is the perfect opportunity to bring their guests together once again. Callie, prepping the salad, turns to Molly and says she hopes the three *couples* will begin a tradition tonight.

"You assume that Alan and I are a *couple*," Molly rebukes her sister.

"Well, are you?"

Molly spreads the croutons evenly on top of the salad, looks up and says, "A *couple* has certain implications."

Callie gets her sister's tone. "Sorry. But we haven't talked in a while about you two, and all I hear about from Tom, when he gets back from playing basketball with Alan, is that you two are meeting a lot."

Molly raises an eyebrow, "What does Tom say, exactly?"

"He says that Alan thinks the world of you and that you are working on the play. Memorizing lines, he says."

"I see." Molly wipes her hands on her apron. "Well, we have gotten to know each other through the play. It's a play about the regrets of two lovers who have missed their chance to really understand how each other feels because they only communicate through writing ... instead of talking to each other. *Love Letters*, that's the title. So as it turns out, Alan and I have found ourselves sharing our own past experiences."

"Oh, really." Callie leans against the counter expectantly.

"Yes. But we are not a *couple*. We are becoming good friends." Molly knows her sister is dying to learn exactly what they are *sharing;* however, just then, Tom strides in.

"What are you talking about, you two?" He then answers his own question. "I'll bet this about my star basketball teammate and my Broadway actress sister-in-law. Well, I just wanna say one thing." He pauses for dramatic effect and then reconsiders his announcement when he sees the expressions on the sisters' faces, which is clear as a flashing yellow warning light: W*atch what you're about to say, Mister!*

Tom croaks, "Maybe this is none of my business, so I'll just go back to the wine."

"No, no, Tommy." This from Callie. "What were you going to say? We're curious. After all, you guys spend a lot of time together doing guy stuff."

"Excuse me. Senior League Recreational Basketball is not 'guy stuff.'"

"No?"

"No. It's a serious, athletic endeavor in which the thrill of victory is pitted against the agony of defeat."

Callie takes two steps toward her husband. "Tom, knock off all the Wide World of Sports crap and just tell us what Alan says about my sister."

Tom throws his hands up in the air. He knows that what he's about to say might get him into trouble. "Okay, okay. Now, this is just my take, but I think Alan is smitten." With that, he turns and tries to exit.

"Oh, no, you don't. You can't just say that and then leave, Tommy." Callie grabs his arm. "What did Alan say that made you come to your crystal ball prediction that he is smitten?"

Molly turns away from the two of them. She isn't interested in their matchmaker routine. She leans down and observes the prime rib roast in the lower oven to see how it is coming along.

Meanwhile, Tom explains, "It's not something he said, it's just the way he talks about Molly. Look. It's a guy thing. I can just tell he likes her."

Molly turns from the oven and faces the two conspirators. "Oh, God. Listen to you two. We aren't in high school. Tom, let me explain something to you ... and to my sister. One, I do like him. He's great. He's very much a gentleman. And, yes, he is very handsome. Two, I am not looking for a knight in shining armor to come save my day. All I'm looking for these days is a sword ... a sword to defend myself. And I'd like the people around me to have my back and not stab something in it."

Tom and Callie stand frozen.

Molly continues, "So, for now, I really just like being with Alan, and it *is* nice to know he enjoys my company. And that is just the way it is." She reaches for the open bottle of red wine, pours a splash, and takes a sip.

With that, Tom nods and slips away, obviously chastised. Callie also looks embarrassed that she has been a co-conspirator. She mutters, "So, I guess the *couple* thing is not appreciated, huh?"

Molly moves to the vegetables that have been prepared for roasting. "I'm sorry, Callie. I didn't mean to jump on you and Tom. I'll make it up to him later. It's just that Alan has a lot of baggage. And so do I."

She seasons and stirs the vegetables, using that time to consider how much to share of what has transpired between her and Alan. "The last time we met, he told me about Sophie's death in the car accident. He has not spoken to many people about it. It was a gut-wrenching time for him. His pain was visceral. I don't know how someone gets through losing the person they love ... suddenly, with no warning." She sighs, "So Tommy may think Alan is 'smitten,' but I feel he's broken. And I'm not here to pick up the pieces and try to glue his heart back together. I'm not Sophie, and I don't want to be. I am not a replacement. For now, I'm just a friend."

She walks toward her sister. "And I'm just as broken as he is, Callie. Look. I don't have a lifelong partner. I don't even have a house. I'm unemployed. I'm an over-the-hill actress ..."

"No, you're not!"

Not what?"

"Over-the-hill! Or without a home. You have us. And you are not unemployed. You are retired!" That breaks the tension. They burst out laughing, as they have done their entire lives. Then Callie reminds her sister, "Long marriages, big houses and jobs, those are just what society says you should have. You're in a really good place. Not many people can say that."

The doorbell rings. "Thank you. You better see who it is."

Callie goes to the door and calls back, "It's Renee and Patrick with dessert. They always bring a fantastic dessert!"

"Merry Christmas!" Tom yells out from the living room.

"This is such a treat." Patrick is just as loud. "And thank you for hosting!"

Renee steps into the foyer and gets a quick kiss from Tom and a kiss and a hug from both of the sisters. She observes the living room and says, "Oh my. Your decorations are so beautiful." As she strides into the room, she sees the noble fir tree adorned with twinkling white lights, a string of wooden cranberries crisscrossing the width of the tree, and ornaments that are souvenirs from the many travels her hosts have taken over the years.

She pivots to Molly, puts both her hands on Molly's forearms, and eyes her professionally. "Your hair looks fantastic. I love your French braid. Did you do it yourself?"

"Oh, no. That would be impossible for me. I'm too uncoordinated. Callie is the one who has the touch. But thanks, I really like it, too," Molly replies. Then she moves to Patrick, gives him a quick kiss on the cheek and asks him, "How are ticket sales going for the fundraiser?"

Patrick returns the affection, "We're already nearly sold out, and we haven't spent much on advertising. Your name, naturally, is the draw." He pauses, then bows toward her to whisper in her ear. "But there is a slight problem."

Renee sees what Patrick may be up to and steps between the two, "No, Patrick. Not tonight. We can discuss this later." She looks at Molly, "It's just a work-in-progress. No worries." Patrick steps back and acquiesces with a nod.

Molly looks at both of them. "Well, okay, but just so you know, I've been rehearsing with Alan for a month, and we have this play down."

"Oh, that's great," Renee smiles.

"Oh, that's really great!" Patrick is far more enthusiastic than what is called for, which piques Molly's interest in what Renee called a work-in-progress. An awkward moment ensues, interrupted by Tom asking what they want to drink. Just as quickly, Callie asks Renee if she can bring their dessert into the kitchen. Renee follows her but keeps an eye on her husband.

All this scuttle leaves Molly alone momentarily with Patrick. She prods him, "Come on. What's the problem? It can't be too bad."

Patrick keeps his voice down, "Okay, look. I'll tell you, but let's just sit on it for now."

"Fine." Molly is stubborn. "What?"

"The actor I lined up to play Andy ... he just called me and told me he has to back out. He said he felt terrible about it, but something important has come up in L.A."

Molly knows what that implies. She rolls her eyes. "An audition."

"Yep. Something big. He told me if I'm in a jam, he can find someone to step in."

"Of course. It's always something big." Molly cuts him off. *An idea comes to her.* She looks behind her to see if the others are within earshot. They're not. So, she says, "No. Don't get somebody else. I'll explain later. Let's not talk about this now. Let me handle it. I'll call you, okay?" She looks over her shoulder again and sees Renee coming into the living room with Tom.

Molly exits to the kitchen to help Callie toss and plate each salad. Tom pops the cork on his patio and then comes into the kitchen to fetch the champagne flutes. Just then, the doorbell rings. The door is slightly ajar, and Alan enters with a lovely bouquet of red and white roses and something in the shape of a wine bottle wrapped in silver and gold paper. "Hello, everyone. Merry Christmas!" he calls out.

Callie takes the flowers from his hands. "Oh, Alan, these are gorgeous. Thank you so much." Tom sidles up to him, squeezes his shoulder and remarks, "Is that the wine we had at your place the other day? It was fantastic." Alan nods.

Molly waits for her turn at the end of what has become a greeting line while Renee and Patrick, not for the first time, thank Alan for all he has done to help them this year with the theater. Renee whispers something to Patrick and nods toward Molly. Patrick gets the not-so-subtle hint, grins and announces, "Cue Molly."

Molly steps forward with her arms out, "There is my co-star," she beams.

Alan reaches for her, "Oh, no. I'm just making sure she knows her lines."

"You've been more like an understudy," Molly says as she quickly kisses him on the cheek.

They pull apart, smiling, and for the first time gaze into each other's eyes. Again, Molly looks over at the others, and when she sees they're distracted, she whispers, "I have something to ask of you. Can we talk later?"

Alan says in a hushed voice, "Of course. Coincidentally, I have something to ask you, as well."

Molly steps back, surprised. "Ah, mysterious are we. Well, it's Christmas, so it is a time of giving, isn't it?"

"It most certainly is."

Two hours pass with lively banter about plans for the next season with the theater, books each of them loved, concerts they attended and those they hope to go to, the lack of good movies to see, and the need to make sure they enjoy each other's company more often. Nat King Cole's "Chestnuts Roasting on an Open Fire" and Johnny Mathis' "It's Beginning to Look a Lot Like Christmas" accompany the conversation.

The beef tenderloin roast, scalloped potatoes, and grilled vegetables drizzled with truffle oil are savored by all. After enough time has passed, legs are stretched, dishes cleared, and coffee is served with the thin slices of black forest cake that Renee's favorite French bakery, Isabelle's, has provided.

Molly taps her spoon on her coffee cup. "Everyone. I know it's past the time for the usual toast to be made, but this Christmas Eve dinner is a first for me here in my old hometown with wonderful friends and family. So I just want to express my gratitude to my kid sister ..."

"... by four minutes," injects Callie.

"And her kinda, okay husband, Tommy," laughter ripples down the table, "and to my new friends who have opened their theater to me. And last but not least, my counselor and *Love*

*Letter* reading partner, Alan. He has patiently, as you all have, helped me reclaim my hometown. Thank you all so much."

Cheers are followed by Tom's pronouncement: "Thank you all for coming and ... 'To all a good night!'" With that, coats and purses are retrieved, and farewells are given out. Final hugs and kisses are exchanged.

Renee and Patrick are the first to exit. Alan seems ready to leave but hesitates when Molly touches his arm and tells him to wait so she can chat with him. She heads back to the kitchen and makes sure Callie doesn't have too much on her hands. Tom and Callie shoo her away, saying they have everything under control.

Alan helps her with her coat. Molly says her goodbyes, and Callie reminds her to come by tomorrow to see her nieces and nephews. She and Alan leave together, stepping into the cold, foggy air.

It takes only a few steps for Molly to realize just how cold it is on this Christmas Eve. Her car is in Callie's driveway; Alan's is further down the street, so Molly touches Alan's arm and says, "Can we sit in my car for a quick chat?"

"Of course. It's pretty chilly tonight."

Settling in, Molly smiles, hoping that *chilly* is not how Alan will receive her ask. She decides to get right to the point. "Alan, I'm going to ask something, and I want you to know that I don't expect an answer now. I want you to think about it, okay?"

"Sure."

"Good. Here's the scoop. The actor who is playing opposite me just bailed, and Patrick told me tonight. Typical flighty actor. Anyway, I would like for you to think about stepping into the role of Andy. Before you say anything, Patrick can always get another actor—he told me that—but I asked him to wait because, and I am being totally honest here, I think you are really good. More importantly, you and I have a connection. We have the timing down, and that's so important in this play because of all the quick back-and-forth banter."

Alan waits.

Molly stares at him, "You're doing that thing."

"What thing?"

"When you listen."

"Is that a problem?" Alan asks.

"No. No. It's ... one of the many things I really like about you. But I'm wondering what your reaction is because, damn, you have a great poker face."

Alan explains, "Oh. Well. I wasn't sure you were finished."

"Okay. You need to stop being so thoughtful." Nervous laughter from Molly.

"Well, *are* you finished?"

"No. I also want to say that I promised you would never have to be on the stage, and you were clear about not wanting to be. So I'm feeling guilty now asking you and breaking my promise, but ... damn it, Alan, you've got it. You totally understand Andy, and when you read, you make me leave myself and become Melissa. And you have no idea how powerful that is. Okay, now I'm done." She slumps behind the steering wheel.

Alan takes a breath. "I'm flattered. Very flattered. And I'm glad you think I could pull this off, but I am going to take your advice and think about it. Unfortunately, the performance is in four days, so I need to make up my mind pronto."

"True. Yes."

Alan looks out the window. "Maybe having so little time is better on my nerves. I'm going to sleep on it ... if I can."

"Good. Good. Wait." Molly again reaches for his arm. "You said you had something to ask me. What is it?"

Alan returns his gaze to her. "Oh. Right. I'm glad you reminded me. So, long story short, for the last fifteen years, my firm has sponsored and served meals at our local church hall to seniors and people in need. We get a large turnout from many folks in North County. If you have the time tomorrow, I know, last minute, so you can bow out, no worries. But would you come with me and help serve meals? I think it will put you in the Christmas spirit. It always does for me. See, with Zoey out of town, we could ... I could use a helping hand."

Molly pivots in her seat so she is directly facing him. "Oh, Alan. Of course. I'd love to. When?"

"Great. It's from four o'clock to six."

"Perfect! I'll be at Callie's before that, and then, what? Should I meet you at your house?"

"Yes. Look, I'm very grateful you can pitch in, and ..." he hesitates. "And then I won't be ... by myself.*"*

Molly lets that admission have its moment. Then she decides to follow his lead.

"Me, too." She leans toward him and kisses him tenderly.

# Act 4:
# The Promise

## Act 4, Scene 1:
## Molly's Christmas Day

Molly watches nervously. Alan has frozen in front of a full house. The audience leaves, flying away from their seats like angels. Patrick holds the door to the theater closed. No matter. The angels float past him. Then abruptly, Molly herself appears in black and white in a scene from the Christmas classic "It's a Wonderful Life," and the stars in the heavens begin shaking their heads and gossiping about poor Alan Bernstein. She sees Alan trudging through snow toward an icy bridge. He's on the bridge. He's about to jump! She screams, "No! You can't, Alan. I'm here. Don't you see me?" Suddenly, the angels are transformed back into townsfolk and are clamoring back into the La Paloma Playhouse, rushing to the concession stand. Renee is pleading with them that she doesn't have enough money to give them a refund. Molly rushes into the lobby screaming, "It's all my fault! I made him do it. He wasn't ready!"

Molly shakes herself awake. Her nightgown is soaked in sweat. The wine, the dinner, the late night, Alan's trepidation about being on stage in four days, all of it blurred into one nonsensical dream. An actor's nightmare, revisited!

She sits up, jabs her fingers into her hair. *Oh, my God, Molly. Keep it together!* She looks at the clock. *Oh no, it's 8:45 already!*

She reaches for the phone to call Alan, but before she can dial his number, she notices she has a voicemail. Figuring it must be Alan, she clicks to listen to the voice she most wants to hear. Instead, it's Leo. She hits pause and considers if she wants to listen to Leo right now. The call was made at 8:00 last evening when her phone was tucked away in her coat. *What is he calling me for on Christmas Day!* She clicks to continue the message.

"Hey, you remember me? Your agent, Leo! Long time no hear. Anyway, my people—who used to be your people, too—let me know that you're performing in a play! What gives? I thought you were through with the acting business. You remember what you told me? You were done. So then, I find out it's a fundraiser for some friends, and it's at some community theater. Okay. I get it. No more casting couch drama, which, you remember, I helped you deal with back then. So anyway, no hard feelings about ignoring my calls. But I do have good news for you. I've had inquiries about your availability—that's right. And better yet, I'm coming down to see you. Yep. I'll be in the audience at ... what's it called? Oh, yeah, the La Paloma Playhouse. Maybe we can talk then, huh? Look, I'll be staying the night down there, and I hope you'll contact me. You know, I have always been in your corner. Love ya, kid. Merry Christmas."

Molly erases the message and mutters to herself, "How can I ever get off this rollercoaster ride?"

At 10:00, she scoots down to the Italian bakery on India Street to grab some pastries she promised to bring over to Callie's as a treat for her nephew and niece, along with the gifts she's bringing for all the family. As she walks by the front window, she sees the four bocce ball boys at one of the tables sipping what is left of their espressos.

"Merry Christmas, boys!" she proclaims as she steps into the bakery. They all stand. She moves to each one and gets a peck on the cheek.

"Ah, our *bella donna*. That was my Christmas wish!" says Big Sal, who has removed his black fedora and placed it over his chest.

Sergio, the leader—the former priest—is next. "We missed you at bocce ball last week."

"Yeah," Rudy, his younger brother, the one with the permanent five o'clock shadow, chirps. "They cheat when you not there."

"Boys. Boys. I know you all cheat all the time, but it's Christmas, so I forgive you. I've been busy," Molly explains.

"Okay. Good. We go to Mass at noon. You come with us?" Sergio asks. Molly shakes her head indicating no.

Rudy tells her, "We all pray we make it another year!"

"Well, of course you will!" Molly tells them, "You are still young ... and Italian!" They all nod. "Are you boys seeing family later?"

Big Sal and Geno look at the brothers. "We have Christmas with Sergio and Rudy's family," says Geno, brushing his hand over his silver goatee. "Next year, we go to San Francisco, all of us, to stay with my family. We mix it up."

"Me," Big Sal admits, "I am alone. My wife, Nina, she die almost five years. We have no kids. So these guys, they adopt me."

"Sergio turns to Molly, "What about you, Molly, you have a place to go? You can come to my house if you want."

"Yeah. You sit in the backseat with me and Big Sal." Geno is all smiles.

"Oh, no, boys. No backseat with any of you characters." They all laugh knowingly. "Look, I'm grabbing some goodies and heading to my sister's to see her family and my father."

Sergio nods, "Ah. Your Papa. Good girl. Very nice. Always love your Papa," he advises.

"Yes, of course, but I want to tell you boys something I think you'll enjoy. I am inviting you to be my guest to see a play I am performing. My treat. I will get you tickets."

"A play?" Sergio repeats.

"You in a play?" Big Sal isn't sure he heard right.

Geno slaps his head. "Don't you listen? Yes. She's famous actress. Like Sophia Loren. We looked you up, Molly O'Toole. Well, Sergio's kids did. They show us you on the computer. Very famous!"

Sergio whispers, "Beautiful then. And now." The others nod enthusiastically.

Molly smiles, accepting their compliments. "Okay. Thank you. Here's the poster for the show." She has one folded in her purse. "I'm glad I saw you today because I was going to find you at the park. I really hope you come. The play is called *Love Letters.*"

Rudy can't help himself. "Is it sexy?"

Sergio pushes him, "Shuddup! Molly is classy woman. You still need to grow up."

"No sex, boys. Lots of love, though. Look, here's my cell, Sergio. Text me or call to tell me if all four of you are coming so I can save seats, okay?"

Geno erupts, "No. You can't give him you phone number. No fair. No, he will brag about having the number of beautiful, young actress!"

"Okay. Look," Molly takes three other napkins and jots down her number for the others. She quickly orders pastry, turns to them and waves. "Merry Christmas! Ciao!" She leaves just as quickly, but glances back through the window and sees the four men holding their napkins with her number like they've been blessed by an angel. She blows them a kiss.

Today will be all about family, Molly tells herself, and then can't help but smile. There were so many years when she was on the road or otherwise involved in relationships with men and their families. Now, she's grateful for the opportunity to bring pastries to her niece and nephew and share lunch with her own family.

Next on this day is a visit to the oldest member of the family. Liam's senior care facility has been decked out with holiday decor, and the memory care wing has its share of festive decorations, with the staff dressed as Santa's helpers.

Liam is in his room wearing his red Christmas sweater. He can't remember anybody's name today, but he's enthusiastic about seeing them all, anyway. He sits up straight long enough for presents to be opened, but almost immediately after that falls asleep in his chair. He's snoring by the time they all tiptoe out of his room.

While the rest of the family heads out for a beach walk, Callie and Molly drift outside to sit on the bench that just a few months ago was the scene of their father's fall.

It's quiet for a moment, and then Callie breaks the spell. "It's Christmas."

"Yes."

"So. I think you were—I'm not going to use the word *couple*—but you would have to be blind to not notice that Alan has given you a lot of attention."

Molly touches her sister's hand. "I know. God, I wish he was a jerk so I could just not get involved with him ... but then I'm pinching myself because finally I've met a decent gentleman. He's really a good guy."

Callie nods vigorously. "Yeah, he is. And he's easy on the eyes, too."

Molly smiles. "This is true. But you don't know the latest."

"Oh?"

"Last night, Patrick told me that the actor playing opposite me in the play flaked out."

"No."

"Yes."

Callie's eyes bug out. "Wait. I did see you and Patrick being kinda secretive when he first came in. What are you gonna do?"

Molly replies, "Normally, I'd be having a panic attack, but this time, instead, I think I've given Alan one."

"What?" Callie quickly solves the mystery. "Oh. Wait. You think Alan can do the show?"

"I do, but ..."

Callie cuts in, "But *he* doesn't."

Molly winces. "Um. He has serious doubts. More importantly, I promised him he would never be put in this position. That's the agreement we made when he became my practice partner."

"Oh!"

"Oh."

"So. Did you ask him?"

"I did." Molly drops her head into her hands.

"When?"

Molly speaks through her fingers. "In my car when we left your house last night."

"Wow."

"Yeah." Molly raises her head.

"Oh, shit. What did he say?" Callie literally is on the edge of her seat ... or in this case, the bench.

"Well, I told him to not decide right then. But I asked him to think about it. Because Patrick says he can find someone else. And if he doesn't feel comfortable, I understand."

"You do?" Callie looks slightly mortified.

"Yes. Well, no! I'll be heartbroken." Molly looks directly at her sister.

"Because...?"

"Because he is really good and we just connect ... as a man and a woman should."

Quiet again.

Callie offers, "Please tell me that you told him what you just told me. About how you think he's good and how you feel about ... you know ... you two."

Molly nods. "I did. I told him he has *the 'it' factor.* For goodness sake, he's a lawyer. A trial lawyer. He has command." She pauses, "And as for how he feels about me, well, I don't know. Remember, Alan is still grieving Sophie. And he's reserved, Callie. He's difficult to read."

"When will Alan tell you about doing the play? And, maybe while you're having that talk, you might want to find out how he actually feels about you."

Molly collects herself. "That's the thing. He invited me later today to go to the church dinner that his firm has sponsored for years. He asked me if I would help serve the folks dinner. Usually, Zoey helps, but she's out of town with her boyfriend."

"Oh, good for her. She's a doll."

Molly nods.

"You met her, right, at the theater, didn't you?"

Molly nods again.

"Did you get along?"

"Absolutely. We were a team working concessions. We had a chance to talk, too."

Callie makes a proclamation. "My instincts tell me that if Alan talks to Zoey before he talks to you again, then he will say *yes.*"

Molly looks up at the sky. "I hope so, but I also hope he doesn't feel forced because then I'll feel so guilty."

## Act 4, Scene 2:
# Alan's Christmas Day

Alan has been awake since dawn. He, like Molly, tossed and turned much of the night. Nerves. Indecision. Missing Sophie. Missing Zoey. And now, he finds himself missing Molly O'Toole.

At 9 am, Zoey FaceTimes him. She is sitting on a love seat with Dan next to her. *They look so darn happy.*

"Merry Christmas, Dad!"

"Hey, you two. Merry Christmas!"

Zoey exudes joy, "Did you find the Christmas gift I put under the tree?"

Alan stands and carries his laptop with him. "Oh. Let me go over there and look."

"Dad. You are making us dizzy. Just put the computer down for a minute." Zoey rolls her eyes, but Alan doesn't notice.

"Oh. Sorry." Alan finds the package. "Okay. Got it. Let's see." "Ah. It's a book. That much I can tell." He carefully undoes the wrapping paper. "Oh my! *The Tucci Cookbook.* You know how much I love Stanley Tucci. It says 'Great Italian dishes a guy can make'. Well, that's me, all right. Thanks so much."

Zoey beams, "Remember we watched all his specials when he toured Italy last Christmas?'

"Yes."

"So when Dan and I went shopping for a father who has almost everything, we found this book. When we get home, you can try one of Tucci's recipes on us."

Dan makes his debut. "I'm sure it will be great."

Alan smiles at Dan as best as one can on a computer. "Of course it will. And you can open your gifts I have under the tree then, too. So, how has the trip gone?"

Zoey rattles off the highlights so quickly that Dan barely has a chance to inject "It was fantastic" before excusing himself to speak with his folks and give Zoey some privacy with her father.

"So, Dad, how's it going? You had dinner with your friends, and I assume Molly was there, right?"

"Yes. It was a lovely evening. But I got a surprise, and I need to get your opinion ... or at least bounce something off you." Alan settles himself back into the couch, balancing the laptop on his knees.

"What's that?"

He proceeds to explain his dilemma: let Molly down or face the experience he swore he would never agree to. "I really don't think I can do this play, but ..."

Zoey cuts him off, "Look, Dad. Before I left, you told me Molly thinks you're doing great reading the part. You need to trust her. Don't you?"

"Well, she's biased."

"No, she's not. Dad, you are being stubborn."

A pause. Then, "Yeah. I'm pretty stubborn, huh?"

Zoey decides to put her foot down. "Listen, Dad. I have to tell you something. I remember the first time Mom let me come to the courthouse to see you give your closing statement to a jury. I was 12 years old. I was so proud of you. And I was stunned at how you commanded the jury's attention. Your poise. Your confidence. Sure, it took you years to be a great lawyer. But, Dad, you are the reason I am a lawyer, and this is one thing I'm confident you can pull off really well. Look at the audience and pretend they are your jury. You will win. You will."

Alan is speechless. Not because he doesn't know what to say, but because he doesn't want to admit a gut-wrenching truth. I'm telling her the easy part. The part she can understand. The part she witnessed at the funeral. Stoic me. That's what I showed her. She doesn't know what happened to me after she left that day and the days, weeks, months ... all these years since. How terrified I've been. And how embarrassed I'd be to admit that.

"Dad?"

"Yes."

"Dad. You have always talked to me about growth as a person and as a professional. Okay, so this is your time to grow—for yourself. And one more thing. Molly means something to you, and you need to step up and show her that."

Alan's voice breaks, "Okay, Sweety. Okay." He leans closer to the screen. "God, I love you."

"Daddy, I love you, too."

## Act 4, Scene 3:
# Christmas Night

Alan is looking out his front window, where he can see Molly sitting in her car putting on lipstick, brushing her hair, and checking herself in the visor's mirror. She's half an hour early. *She's probably worried about what I'm going to say about being in the play with her. I better put her out of her misery.*

Alan steps out of his front door just as Molly steps out of her car.

"Hey, you. Merry Christmas!" Alan's arms are open for an embrace as he says, "I'm so glad you agreed to help me, even though it is Christmas Day."

"Hey, you. Merry Christmas!" Molly echoes as she moves forward.

Alan steps forward and kisses her. It's a friendly kiss on the cheek. Then, he steps back to assess how she's taking his forwardness and, relieved to see her smile, bends at the waist and hugs her.

Molly looks up at him. "I'm here to help you because you asked and because what you're doing is such a good cause, Mr. Alan Bernstein. I will try my best to fill Zoey's shoes. Speaking of Zoey ..." Molly taps Alan on his forearm and points to her shoes, "Since I have Zoey's shoes to fill today, I put on my tennis shoes. My waitress days, many moons ago, kicked in, and I figured I'd be on my feet for a couple of hours. Oh, have you had a chance to wish Zoey Merry Christmas today?"

"Oh, of course. She and I spoke first thing this morning. She told me she's having a wonderful time with Dan and that his family has been gracious. She'll be back in two days, and we'll spend time together. This time with Dan."

They're still smiling at each other as Alan steps back and motions toward his front door. "Since we're a little early, do you want to come inside for a few minutes?"

He ushers her into the living room and gets her a glass of water, and they sit on the couch. Alan leans forward. "Molly, sometimes in life you have to trust your gut. And so, after thinking about what you asked me to do—*oh, dear, her smile is frozen*—I've decided that ... that I'm going to trust you and hope that you can help pull me through in this play."

Molly gasps in relief. "Oh, my God, Alan! You had me on the verge of a nervous breakdown! Whew! See, I told you that you have a flair for the dramatic." Molly leans in and gives him a kiss. "Alan, you are going to be great. You are not going to regret this. I promise."

His eyebrows rise.

"Oh, gosh. Wrong choice of words. *Promise.* Well, this time, a promise is a promise. Okay?"

Alan laughs, "Relax, Molly. I know how much this means to you. And to Renee and Patrick, and the playhouse. I just hope I'm passable in the part. But I thought we could talk more about it later, after we serve lunch. Unless you have other plans."

"No. I mean, yes! We can—we should—talk afterwards. I've already been to Callie's and visited with her family and spent time with my father. You are the only person on my dance card this evening."

Alan nods. "Same here. Let's get going. I've got some people I'd like to introduce you to at the church. Folks I have known for many years. Okay?"

"Absolutely."

At the church, assigned to waitress duties, Molly experiences what it is like when one is doing the Lord's work. Time flies by, and smiles are genuine. One hears the word "grateful." *It's nice to hear applause in a theater, but there is something so substantially fulfilling about serving a hot meal to someone who needs it. They need not just the meal, but also people to share it with who care for them.*

During a short break, she turns to Alan, "This is one of the most remarkable things I've done on a Christmas Day."

Alan nods. "Yes. I totally get it."

"Thank you for inviting me." She wipes her hands on her apron, which has "A Christmas Bounty of Love" embroidered on it along with the names of the Christmas dinner sponsors. One of those sponsors is the law firm of Zimmerman, Williams and Bernstein.

Alan introduces her to Zimmerman and Williams, both of whom shake hands in friendly fashion and then glance at each other with raised eyebrows.

Molly gathers that Alan hasn't shared much of his recent personal life since retiring.

As soon as Alan tells his former partners that he'll be sharing the stage at the La Paloma Playhouse with the actress Molly O'Toole, both insist on buying up any remaining tickets that haven't been sold. "You can be Atticus Finch speaking to the jury once again," Ron Zimmerman tells him. "Remember how we used to kid you?" And Lucius Williams, the younger partner, chimes in, "We absolutely will not miss this. The entire firm will be there, Alan."

Alan rolls his eyes. A packed house for sure.

Molly sees Alan's dismay. She tugs his arm, whispering, "Don't worry. You won't be able to see them."

Soon, they're serving the last slices of apple pie. Molly takes over dish duty, and Alan moves among the tables, scooping up the rest of the plates and conversing with people whom she thinks may have been church members for many years.

When she's done with the dishes, she steps out of the kitchen and overhears Alan tell an elderly couple, "I get more out of this event than anything I used to do in the courtroom." Molly's eyes widen. She considers what this says about him and how lucky she is that circumstances have brought the two of them together.

They decide they're both hungry, not having taken the time to feed themselves, and Alan suggests they whip up something at his house. On the way, Molly listens to a voicemail from Patrick.

"He wants to know what I have in mind for the play," she tells Alan. "I just told him yesterday to hold off finding someone to play Andy because I had an idea."

"And I am that idea?"

"Yep. A pretty good one, I think. I'll call him and put his mind to rest."

Molly calls Patrick, and the conversation that Alan can hear sounds like this: "Yes. Yes. Of course. I'm very confident. Yes! No, I didn't guilt him into it. No. Yes. Really? I'll ask him. He's sitting right next to me. No, we are not! I'm in his car! Can I call you back? Right," and she punches the off button.

"Patrick asked me ..." She pauses to put things in order. "First, wait, let me tell you that he is excited. And a little surprised, considering you were pretty adamant about never being on stage."

"Okay."

*I love how he lets me explain things and doesn't interrupt. I wish I was that calm.* "So, he wants you to call him when we get in the house. I think he wants to be certain you're good with the decision. I think he also wonders if I twisted your arm." She smiles.

"No problem. He can come over if he wants. Wait, what am I saying? It's Christmas. I'll call him and tell him you were not using undue influence." He smiles back at her.

After that call, and after they've had a salad with some warm sourdough bread, they lean back on the kitchen stools with white wine glasses mostly emptied. They are sitting in the same place they were when they first started rehearsing.

Alan sighs, "This must be one of the most unusual Christmas Days you've spent."

"Oh. There have been crazier ones, with actors and theater drama, but never one as busy or as inspiring as this one. That reminds me, I wanted to share something with you. It's about when you were talking to that older couple as we were wrapping up."

"Oh, no. What did I say?"

Molly puts her finger up in the air. "It's partly what you said, but also what you did. You told them that this event means more to you than any time in a courtroom. Nobody else was within earshot, and you didn't know I was eavesdropping."

Alan pauses, seemingly caught, and then recovers. "Oh. Well, I've known them since the very first dinner we served. Love them dearly."

"Right. I get that." Molly pushes on. "But here's the thing. There's a saying that goes something like, 'One should be doing the right thing, even when no one is watching.'' Look, Alan, in many ways, we don't really know each other all that well. We've never talked about the issues of the day, politics or the things that make us happy or sad. But that moment, you with those folks, helped get me the measure of the man."

Quiet.

Alan nods. "Remember, Molly, you're the one with the apron and dishcloth. You were the one who dropped everything on Christmas to come with me. So the same could be said of you."

He stops, but his pointer finger tapping his lips and his furrowed brow tell her he has something more to say. She does know him that well. *He's worried, nervous, maybe wondering if now is the time to trust me with some secret.*

Then he lays his hand flat on the tabletop and launches in. "Molly, I haven't been honest with you or Zoey and certainly not with myself. I wasn't going to ever speak of this to anyone, but when I talked to Zoey this morning, I knew I have to face what is really troubling me about performing on stage ... and it's not you or the characters in the play."

Molly leans closer. Let him talk. What is it that's so troubling?

He takes a big breath and releases it with three words. "At Sophie's funeral." Another breath, then, "When I lost my wife. I kept everything inside. Closed. I kept a grip on my sorrow. I kept it so tight that I hardly spoke to anyone. When people wanted to go on and on about how tragic it was and how God awful *they* felt ... I just nodded and walked away. As for Zoey, I was determined to show strength. Zoey was so devastated that if I mirrored her ... well, I couldn't do that.

"The moment I saw Zoey's car pull away from the cemetery, I broke. I tried to get away. Somewhere. Anywhere away from people. So they couldn't see me ... couldn't talk to me. Molly, they wanted to hug me, console me. They surrounded me. I guess I had put up such a front. Maybe because the man they knew would never fall apart. And then I just panicked. I was shaking, crying. I couldn't even talk. I remember how much my throat ached. But I couldn't say anything.

"Some of my closest friends saw me break down at the funeral. They saw something so guttural, like they were staring at *my* body in a car wreck. I scared them. I remember thinking, they're gawking at me. I don't know how I eventually escaped. I just pushed the people I loved away. I was somebody else. I couldn't stop crying even when I started my car. The tears blinded me.

He chokes, then stops.

Molly knows how hard this was for him to voice to her. Don't tell him you understand. How could anyone understand?

Alan takes a few breaths. Then, as if coming up for air, he finally tells her. "Later, my reaction to how I'd lost it ... it was so embarrassing. From that day until right now, with you, I have kept my emotions bottled up."

His teeth are clenched. His body is stiff. Sweat on his forehead has beaded up and drifted down his cheeks.

Let it go, Alan.

Alan spits out a confession. "Molly, the truth is that I'm afraid to be on stage in front of some of the same people I know ... who saw me ... because I might lose control."

"Oh, Alan!" Molly bursts into tears, pushes herself off the stool and embraces him. She holds him tight, and he responds in kind. They stay in each other's arms until each of them can slowly relax and melt, melt away from each other. They wipe salty tears from their cheeks.

Nerves. His and mine.

Finally, Alan composes himself to speak, knowing that he can say what he has to say without breaking. "Meeting you, Molly, and acting in the play is helping me have the courage to feel again."

The weight of Alan's emotions moves Molly so much that she has a leap of faith. "Alan, before we met, I wouldn't allow myself to open up and feel vulnerable, either. I didn't trust myself, partly because of my history with cheating husbands and selfish, callous men who have hurt me deeply." *It's time to tell him my truth.*

"Alan," she begins, "Let me tell you my story. When I was a young starlet, I was so invested in my acting, my metamorphosis into the women I played. When I came off the stage ... when I wiped off the grease paint and the wig and got out of my costume ... when I looked into the mirror, what was staring back at me was ... me. But who was I?"

She scoots back on the stool and sits. "Oh, sure, I had a husband then, a family, and I went through the motions of doing things, not taking any time to reflect on what made me happy or fulfilled. All that mattered was how fast I could race to the next audition."

Now it is Alan who listens.

"Then reality hit me full in the face. My marriage ended, and I realized my friends were mirror images of me, desperate for the next show, the next part to play. By then, I had allowed my family to become distant. My sister's family was involved in their kids' world of sports and activities, a life that made me wonder what I was missing. Meanwhile, I just kept chasing after a mirage.

"And once I was 20 years in, I was so invested that I couldn't admit that I didn't know who I was ... other than an actress waiting by the phone for someone to save me.

"Until the day came when, on the set of some god awful commercial for adult diapers, I realized I had sunk so low. So in the middle of the fourth take, I just stopped and walked off the set while the young punk director was yelling at me to 'emote for the camera'! As I walked away, he snarled, 'You are done, O'Toole. Done. I only agreed to work with you as a favor to Leo.'"

Alan looks down. Molly takes a deep breath.

Quiet.

"That punk director, he was an abuser, I know. But that day, I walked away because his voice made me flash back to another time—one that I couldn't *walk away from.* No. I had to scream and punch and run. And ..." Molly's jaw locks. The terror of that night darkens her eyes. "This producer ... this scum ..."

Alan pleads, "Molly, you don't have to ..."

"Yes, I do." She straightens her shoulders. "So many users, vicious and careless. I was, no, I am still so furious. Scarred. When I escaped with my clothes torn and my dreams so ... lost. Well. That's when the despair set in. I felt hollow. I was overwhelmed by emptiness ... But acting was all I'd known. And leaving that world, that life ... that scared me ...*terrified* is a better word."

Alan knows emptiness. Sophie's side of the bed reminds him each night.

Molly looks up at the ceiling. "Alan, when Callie first visited me, a flood of feelings washed over me. Missing events with Callie's kids. Missing milestones with my parents. Missing real relationships with people who want to be with me, not use me. I had a good reason to walk away from my career."

Alan nods. He puts his hand on hers.

She interlocks her fingers with his. "So, Alan, I need to not pull myself together. No. I need to pull myself apart. I've been trying to find out what is my core. I've been asking myself who can I be without all the costumes, the roles, the makeup, the masquerade. That's why I was so scared to do this reading of a play. To walk out on a stage again."

Alan says, "I suppose we are a work in progress, then, huh?"

"Yes, we are. I know I am for sure. But this time I'm playing *me. Molly O'Toole.* I'm going to face the mirror and know myself, and do what really matters. And I want to be with people who have my back, and are not stabbing me in the back."

Molly pivots and leans close. She takes one more deep breath. "Everything you just told me—all of it. You trust me, Alan. Me. Whose heart was so hardened. Who was so cynical.

You've invited me into your world. I hear you pour out your heart to me, and ... and I promise you, we will get through this play together. It will just be you and me reading to each other. Just us. And this play is a chance for us to heal a little. Together. You have helped me so much. But you can't be my salvation, Alan. Maybe you can be a part of it, but it's me who has to do the hard work. I have trust issues that make me keep up walls, and I've been breaking down those walls."

Molly leans back. The anger she's felt for so long, that she can't stand for even a minute longer, is suddenly ... gone.

Alan says very gently, "Now I know *you*, Molly."

They both smile. Molly nods. Funny, how we can hide things so well. Until we can't.

## Act 4, Scene 4:
# The Dress Rehearsal

Alan steps onto the stage. He sees a table finished in natural oak with two matching chairs side by side facing the audience. There are two binders placed on the table in front of each chair with the scripts already set to be read. He's told by Patrick that he will be on Molly's left.

He sits down and looks toward the empty seats in the theater. The bright lights make it so that he can't see past the seats in the front row. That's what Molly said. What a relief.

He glances from side to side, where he can see two green exit signs and not much else. It's far too late for exits.

Molly is in the theater's seats among the empty rows chatting with Patrick and Renee. Even though he can't see them, he can hear them. The acoustics in the theater are such that no microphones are required. Thank goodness. "But you still need to project, Alan," she'd told him as they drove over this morning.

Molly and Renee appear as they step onto the stage. "I talked to Patrick, and we're going to minimize the makeup on you, Alan. He doesn't want you washed out, but I know you would prefer to not have any on."

Renee pipes in, "Really, Alan, just a touch of color for your cheeks, but your good looks will shine through regardless." Her smile is reassuring.

"Okay, that's fine. Is what I'm wearing what you want, Renee?" He is decked out in a crisp white long-sleeved shirt, a charcoal gray suit vest and matching slacks. His jacket will be put on the back of his chair. During the play, he'll wear a red bowtie.

"Alan, you look great," Molly tells him as Renee nods approvingly.

"So are we going to do a run-through now?" Alan asks. His knee is bouncing up and down, so Molly sits next to him and places her hand gently on it to settle him.

"Yes. Only Patrick, Renee and the two crew people will be here for the sound and lighting check and to give us some feedback. Let's try to go through the two acts without stopping, just like we've done at our houses. Remember, our scripts are right here, and we'll turn the pages as we go. Okay?" Without waiting, she turns toward the seats. "Patrick, we're ready."

Patrick's voice comes from the far back row of the theater. "Great. Alan, I'll be introducing you and Molly before you begin, but first, I'll be thanking the audience for their support. Right when I'm done, we will cue the music, which will play for only about a minute while you two come from the wings to your chairs. It'll be dark, so Molly will lead you by the hand. She'll be able to spot the lighted tape on the floor behind the chairs, which helps actors find their places on a dark stage. You'll have plenty of time to settle yourselves. The crew won't bring the lights up until you're in place."

"You can expect the audience to be applauding while you find your chairs," says Renee.

They run through this procedure. Alan hears the song they've chosen for Act One: Frank Sinatra's "My Funny Valentine." Molly intertwines her fingers in Alan's, and in the darkness, they slowly reach their chairs. When he feels Molly's fingers, a sense of calm travels up from his fingers to his arm to his shoulders, and he takes a deep breath. Then the music fades, and the lights come to life. They begin just as they have numerous times before.

Act One is lighthearted, and Alan notices that Molly has increased her energy level. He is drawn to watch her because she is so dynamic. *She is in performance mode. I'm just hanging on for dear life.*

That is when he makes his first mistake. He glances her way during her monologue about where her parents have sent her for the summer. Molly's character is both comically hysterical and sarcastic, and her performance is so energetic that Alan breaks out in laughter. This wouldn't be a problem, except he forgets to turn the page in his script. When he looks down, he delivers the last line on what should be the previous page, and this leads Molly back to the same cue for the same monologue.

*Oh, no! I've messed up!* Alan panics, but before he can break character, Molly comes up with a shorter version of her summer vacation, and does so with such aplomb that an audience wouldn't even notice the repetition. Alan regroups, turns the page, and they get right back to where they're supposed to be.

When they finish Act One, Alan immediately apologizes to Molly. "You saved me there. I was so into your performance that I forgot that I was in the play! You were great and, boy ... anyway ... that will not happen again."

"Alan, that's why we have this rehearsal. We work out the kinks and, in a way, it's my fault because I did my lines differently, leaning into the humor, and that threw you off. You don't need to worry," Molly reassures him.

"Why is that?" Alan is curious.

"Because I know both your lines and mine. That's why, even if there is a slipup, the audience won't even notice. Whatever happens, we are going to be good. She puts out her palm, and he high-fives her.

Patrick and Renee come up to their table. Patrick gushes, "You two are killing it. Renee and I were amazed how well you guys play off each other." *So, even the theater owners didn't notice the slipup. Surely the audience wouldn't have.*

Alan responds, "I'll let Molly take all the credit. Isn't she something?"

Renee continues with instructions. "During the intermission, the lights will fade down, and Molly will lead you backstage, Alan. I'll be there to make sure your makeup is okay, and if you're perspiring, I'll take care of you. I know the lights are very hot."

Patrick follows, "Right. Depending on how much time the audience needs to get refreshments, use the facilities, or just want to talk among themselves, we will judge when to start Act Two. So just relax and regroup. Molly, you'll hear the music play, and about a minute after it starts, we'll dim the lights. That will be your cue to lead Alan back. Let's practice that with the music now, if you both are ready, or better yet, let's give you both a chance to stretch your legs and do whatever you need to do. Okay?"

Both Molly and Alan stand. He's still nervous, but not quite so much. The stage is not a courtroom, but the table could be his defense table, the rows of seats could be the jury box, and the performance is not so different from the drama inherent in any criminal trial.

Sinatra's wishful song, "Someone to Watch Over Me" introduces Act Two. It changes the play's mood from youthful promise to the regrets that come from poor choices and character flaws. Regrets that demand attention and forgiveness. It is in this portion of the play that Alan bears down and tries not to let his mind conjure up memories of his own personal tragedy. He is mostly successful until he comes to the play's tragic ending.

Molly can hear his voice strain and grow hoarse. She picks up the pace so they don't wallow in either character's misery longer than necessary. However, she knows he is struggling to keep his emotions in check and remain in character—in his character's character—rather than drowning in his own pent-up grief.

Focus. Let some emotion out. Release the pressure. Breathe.

The play ends with the characters turning to face each other. For Molly and Alan, it is a release of emotion that is visceral. When the lights go completely out, they hug each other with all their might. Molly whispers, "I'm so proud of you."

Neither of them hears the applause from Patrick and Renee. All they can hear is the beating of their own hearts.

## Act 4, Scene 5:
# Ladies and Gentlemen

Molly parks in Alan's driveway. She's wearing blue jeans and a pink long-sleeve top with a baby blue scarf covering her hair. Her jean jacket is draped over her shoulders. Her garment bag, which Alan assumes contains her dress for the performance, is hanging on the hook in the back seat. She has a bounce in her step and a broad smile on her lips. It is her idea to meet at Alan's and drive together.

She knows that this evening will bring excitement and jitters. There will be distractions, people wishing both of them luck, and as always when a production is on its debut, superstitions that something might go wrong. Alan will need to be kept steady and focused.

Alan is wearing black corduroy pants and a burgundy mock turtleneck. Like Molly, he has his suit and tie in a garment bag and will also hang it in her car. She said they should change at the theater so that when the show ends, they can slip back into their comfortable clothes.

Earlier, he went to the barber shop to get a trim since his hair was beginning to get too long, and during rehearsal, he'd found himself brushing it back off his forehead.

It's still more than two hours before the curtain rises, and the two decide to have a light meal together, a salad much like the one they had when they began this endeavor. The same wine and bread.

"I am a little superstitious," Alan admits. Molly nods knowingly. He proposes a toast, "To no regrets and exciting times ahead." Their glasses touch, and they let this moment linger.

Molly smiles at him. Oh my.

They drive to the theater in Molly's car, which is so old that it has a CD player. She glances over at Alan and says, "This is my favorite Christmas song." She pushes the play button, and Amy Grant's version of "It's the Most Wonderful Time of the Year" fills the air.

She parks the car across the street from the La Paloma Playhouse an hour before curtain. Plenty of time to get Alan ready and not too much time to allow his nerves to get the better of him.

Alan carefully dons his suit, making sure the vest covers his belt. When he begins to try to tie his red bowtie, he realizes his hands are shaking. He's refusing to acknowledge his nervousness, but his body doesn't lie.

Fortunately, Renee comes to the rescue. "Okay, Alan, are you ready for my 'Flawless Touch'? I'm going to put a little makeup on you now." Renee smiles into the mirror, using his reflection to gauge his state of mind.

"I suppose so." He holds the limp bowtie in his hand, "I guess it's better that I didn't tie this." He fails to mention that he couldn't.

"Correct. Let me start with a very light powder on your forehead and such. See, the lights will cause you to sweat a bit and you will have a glow that comes from that. A little rouge will help keep you from washing out."

"Right. I may be washed up but not washed out," Alan chuckles.

Renee touches his shoulders and feels him relax. She delicately adds, "And just a touch of lip gloss ... okay, I'm fibbing, it's lipstick. The audience needs to see your fabulous smile." Renee knows less is best for someone who is new to this business. "See, there." She steps back and looks into his mirror. "Alan, that wasn't too bad, was it?" She winks.

"Oh, it's fine. Fine. But I'm having trouble with my bowtie. My hands are a little ... twitchy."

Renee touches his shoulders again. "Of course they are. That's to be expected. You know, once you start reading the play, those nerves will disappear. Don't worry, I can tie this perfectly." And in less than a minute, the bowtie is sitting perfectly under Alan's chin. Renee combs his hair and puts a dab of holding cream on it, then steps in front of him and says, "Oh, Alan. You will have the ladies in the palm of your hands."

Alan rolls his eyes. "My sweaty palms, Renee." He then stands, hugs her, and ventures into the wings of the stage where he can peek at the audience. The theater seats are nearly all full, the crowd is enthusiastic, and the conversation is animated. It's a live crowd, as they say.

Alan feels a hand gently slide between his shoulder blades. He turns.

He smiles at his co-star. Oh my.

Molly stands silhouetted by the bluish back lights from the far corner of the backstage. She shimmers from the glow that surrounds her petite form.

Alan reaches out to her, and she takes his hand and guides him into the glow of the backlight. Now, he can see her more clearly.

Molly is wearing an off-white knee-length dress with elbow-length sleeves and a red belt that accentuates her waist. She wears a delicate gold necklace and matching earrings. However, it is her hairstyle that draws his attention. Renee has styled it to look like the voluminous and elegant hairstyles worn in the 1940s, She touches a curl and slowly twirls around.

"What do you think?"

"I ... I am ..." Alan stammers. *What should I say? She's stunning.* "I think that you look like ... like a star."

She finishes her turn. "Ha ha," she says, "that's funny because when I asked Renee to style my hair, she wondered what I wanted it to look like. I told her that I am going for the style of Ingrid Bergman's hair when she was in the movie *Casablanca*. You know, when she walks into Rick's American Cafe ..."

Alan finishes her sentence, "... as Ilsa Lund."

"Exactly. She trimmed a bit of my length and with the help of curling irons ... voila." Her smile is infectious.

"Well, you look perfect. And I guess I'm the lucky guy whose gin joint you just walked into." They move toward each other at the same time.

Molly puts her hand on his cheek, caressing him. And then ... their kiss is joy after loss, pleasure after pain. Their kiss is the whole world ahead of them.

Their hearts are beating at a different pace. Molly's is excited, but Alan's is calm. When they step back and look into each other's eyes, they know they are ready for this moment.

Molly quickly freshens her lipstick and then does the same for Alan. As the lights dim, they focus on the stage, where Patrick is speaking.

"Ladies and Gentlemen. My name, for those whom I have not met, is Patrick Swanson. My wife, Renee, and I welcome you. We are the owners of the La Paloma Playhouse, and we will be your hosts for this special event tonight, the reading of A.R. Gurney's Pulitzer Prize-winning play, *Love Letters*.

"Before I introduce you to tonight's guest performers, I would like to tell you how much your attendance means to the both of us. As you may know, the pandemic put our theater, and so many public places, in jeopardy. In the last two years, we have come back from that darkness. This event, here at the end of the year, will put us back on solid financial footing. So we are very grateful for your support and generosity.

"*Love Letters* was first performed in 1988, but it is set in the late 1930s. It has been performed by many famous duos. Tonight, we are fortunate to have two of our local heroes who will graciously step onto our stage to perform this reading. One of them is Molly O'Toole, who has graced the Broadway stage in numerous productions, including the musical *Hairspray* and films like *Groundhog Day* as well as television shows like *The West Wing*. Ms. O'Toole has come back to Encinitas to help support our theater. The other will be making his first, and he insists only, appearance here. He is Alan Bernstein, former barrister celebrated for his commitment to justice, and now a philanthropist who has dedicated his efforts to helping us to restore the grandeur of the La Paloma Playhouse.

"Please enjoy tonight's reading of *Love Letters*." The light dims.

The music begins to play, and Molly holds Alan's hand as they step onto the pitch-black stage. They make their way to their chairs while Frank Sinatra's "My Funny Valentine" is heard throughout the theater. The music fades then, and Sinatra's voice becomes a whisper.

Alan looks up into the white lights and utters the first words that will begin their journey together.

## Act 4, Scene 6:
## And Then ...

Alan has just read Andy Ladd's last letter to his one love, Melissa Gardner, not knowing how he will live without her. Molly, performing as Melissa, delivers her final lines, telling him that he must endure and thanking him for his undying love.

As the stage lights slowly dim, the audience hears the first few bars of Billy Joel's melancholy song "And So It Goes" played on piano. Billy Joel touches the keys softly and deliberately. The song is pensive. Just as he begins to sing, the lights go out on Molly and Alan.

"And So It Goes" reminds the audience that a wounded heart, pained by love's regrets or slashed in tragic loss, can be healed and made strong. That the heart can find its rhythm again. That with patience and a willingness to love, a new love will come.

The audience is hushed. This moment of music and poetry has moved the play from past to present.

Then, in a flash of light, Molly and Alan appear, standing and holding hands in front of the table where their scripts remain, the pages turned to the end. The brilliant lighting cues the audience. As if pulled by a force that they cannot explain, they rise to their feet with affection for the two singular figures. Their applause rises like a wave and becomes a crescendo. Everyone is smiling.

Alan steps back, releasing Molly's hand to encourage the audience to acknowledge her performance. It is she who has turned the play's bittersweet ending to triumph.

Molly steps forward, but only for a moment, because she knows that without her partner, Alan, there never would have been *Love Letters*. She reaches back and pulls Alan forward, allowing him to have his moment. As they come together for a final bow, Renee appears from the wings with a bouquet of red roses for Molly.

From the back of the theater, voices billow in Italian accents. "Bella Donna," "Bellissimo," "Bravo!" Molly waves to her four gentlemen. She can see her sister Callie wiping away tears of joy from her cheeks. Then, she spots Leo, who is standing under the exit sign. He is applauding, but she can see his disappointment at what could have been. Molly makes eye contact but brushes away that foolishness.

Molly lifts Alan's hand, and they take a final bow.

As the two of them turn to each other and embrace, their images become shadows.

And then they vanish.

# Acknowledgements

In the seventeen years since I published my debut novel *Meetings at the Metaphor Café*, I have had a small, scrappy team who have guided me in my own second act from a public school teacher to an author.

In the spirit of the theater, it is time for them to come out for a "curtain call." First, my editor and book designer, Katharine Valentino has diligently and patiently guided this novel with sage advice and a keen eye, keeping me focused on what matters. She also doubles as the cover designer, so she deserves my vigorous applause.

For this novel, I turned to a new friend who traveled with my wife Pam and me into the villages of Italy, Bonnie Halle. She helped me understand how Molly feels as a woman who has faced obstacles and despite all the disappointments, has surfaced stronger and wiser. Besides, Bonnie is from New Jersey, and therefore she and I are "Born to Run."

With a new friend helping me, I also turned to my oldest and newly retired friend Mark McWilliams. Those of you who have followed my writing know that Mark has been my collaborator ever since we worked together in 1979 on the first readers theater, "Whitewash." I have never stopped pestering him for advice, and he has never stopped encouraging me to "find my own voice."

Bonnie and Mark were the yin and yang of my vision for this novel. Often, they set me straight when I wandered into the woods. Without them, I could never have been able to write as well about the loneness and challenges that often accompany "our golden years." Again, they deserve my heartfelt applause.

Also new to our team is Dana Fares, herself an accomplished actress, whose insights into the world of the working actress helped me create the portrait of Molly

O'Toole. Her knowledge helped me to understand the struggles and compromises women often have to face when trying to make it in "show biz." I appreciate her willingness to share what life is like behind the curtain. In so doing, she gave my novel its authenticity. Take a bow, Miss Fares.

I am blessed with an entourage of friends who have helped promote my work and create a platform for an independent author. They include Sandy Gonnerman, Faye Visconti, Joyce Daubert, Karen Harkins Slocomb, Robin Blalock Falcone, and Monique Lampshire Tamayoshi. Michelle Nguyen has been my advisor with social media and has helped me launch video book club chats. Together, they all have a hand in pushing me in front of audiences and being behind the scenes during my journey. Thank you all.

Finally, my wife Pam, a native of Robert Frost's Vermont, patiently listened to me explain this crazy idea that I would write a novel in four acts. When I reached a crossroad and needed her wisdom, she advised me to choose "the road less traveled by and that made all the difference."

I would be remiss to not mention the poignant work of A. R. Gurney, the playwright of *Love Letters*, which was a finalist for the Pulitzer Prize for Drama. If you have a chance to see the play performed, please do not pass up the chance … because you'll regret it, and regrets are what drives his play's characters, Andy and Melissa. Once I read *Love Letters*, I knew that it would be the perfect vehicle for *The Revival of Molly O'Toole*.

# Excerpt from Meet Me at Moonlight Beach

3:00 p.m. On the front steps of Lewis' apartment near San Diego State University.

Lewis has been waiting for forty-five minutes. He knows her comings and goings, but once she has disappeared into her cramped, first-floor studio apartment, he has no chance. She's been there for five months, and not once has Lewis seen one guy clinging to her, which he thinks is hard to fathom—unless she's so ridiculously shy that she just never talks to anyone.

At least he knows her name: Lotte. He ponders the strange name *Lotte, is it short for Charlotte—like the web? Who names their daughter that? No wonder she goes by Lotte.* He also knows she is a business major in her junior year. That's all he could get out of her last week. He's tried the "Hi, how are you?" routine and the "Wanna grab some coffee?" line to no avail.

So he waits on the front stoop of their apartment building.

\* \* \*

Most San Diego State girls seem to fit the stereotype: long blonde hair that is rarely natural, tanned from hours at the beach, and extremely social at "Happy Hour," as well as weekly sorority and fraternity parties. In sharp contrast, Lotte's hermitic life matches her modestly well-worn apparel. Not that Lewis really cares much about girls' wardrobes. Like most twenty-one-year-old seniors, Lewis stirs for what lies underneath the baggy SDSU sweatshirt and the torn-at-the-knees jeans. Lotte's hair is chocolate brown and curly. Her runner's tan reveals toned legs and arms, and to Lewis Bennett, this is merely one reason to be intrigued.

Lotte runs and runs. Every day. Her Sony Walkman is her only companion. Lewis thought about trying to run with her, or at least asking her if that would be okay. But judging from the time he sees her leave to the time he sees her return—all from his third-floor window next to the kitchen—he knows his ego could not withstand the obvious: she would leave him panting on the pavement. Being on the "sports beat" this year for the university's newspaper does not an athlete make.

Finally, she becomes a tiny figure in the distance. Lewis' palms begin to moisten. He has an ace up his sleeve, but he knows that means little if Lotte won't even ante up to the game. She approaches, and it is apparent that she is slowing down, then walking, finally she notices Lewis.

She stops fairly close to him and pulls her curly hair back again so the ponytail is tighter. She is catching her breath. The Walkman has been disconnected.

"Whew."

Lewis thinks, *She speaks!*

"Good run?"

"Great. Started out hot but better now." Her breath is still choppy and her face is flushed, but like many young women, she is not perspiring noticeably. "You locked out?"

"No." Lewis decides it's now or never. "No, I am just sitting here waiting for you."

"What? What did—did I do something wrong? I *did* pay this month's rent, right?"

"Lotte, um, no, no. I'm not a rent collector. I was waiting to ask you something."

"Oh, okay—um, what?" Lewis senses this is *not* going to be easy. There has been no small talk. None of the usual conversation that two college students living two floors apart may have. Lotte is all business.

"Well, you know, I thought about asking you if you wanted a running buddy."

"Yeah..." Lotte shifts her weight to one side and looks askance as young girls are apt to do when they are impatient for a point to be made.

"Okay, well, like, there is no way I could possibly keep up with you."

Lotte laughs. "No, duh."

Lewis understands its implication: *Of course, you can't possibly keep up with me.* But he persists. "So I was wondering if you wanted to see a movie about running? *Chariots of Fire* is playing just down the street, and I heard it's great. You know, a true story about the—"

"Wait, Lewis. Yeah, I know what it's about. But what is *this* about?" She's challenging him.

"Lotte, I'm just asking if you want to go to the movies." Lewis repeats the obvious.

"So, like, on a date?" She is taken off guard by what would be apparent to most young women.

"Um, we could call it that. We could also just call it: 'Lewis asks Lotte if she wants to stop studying and have a nice time eating popcorn and watching other people run—with triumphant music in the background.'"

"Oh, um—I think—well...okay, I guess. Um, I have to tell you something a little embarrassing." Lotte begins to act as if she should stretch her hamstrings out. One leg then the next. Lewis can't help but notice how lovely her legs are.

"Wait," Lewis can't contain himself, "so that's a *yes* on the movie—date thing?"

Lotte takes a big breath and hesitates.

Lewis is befuddled by this adorable, obviously smart girl. Then his mind comes to a dead stop. *Embarrassing? Why?*

"Yes, yes, on the movie date thing, but—" Lotte looks over his head so as not to make eye contact. "I have no money, and I can't pay you back. Well, eventually I can, but—"

"Lotte, we're all poor. It's not a big deal. We'll go to the early show. It's four bucks. We'll sneak in food. Seriously, is that what you are so weird—" he winces as the word comes out and quickly corrects his ill-advised vocabulary, "I mean, nervous about?" He hopes he didn't blow it.

"I know, *weird* is probably the right word. Listen, Lewis, you are nice. I mean, I know you have been giving me hints that you want to get to know me. But you *don't* know me, and if you did, then you would understand why I am the way I am. Okay?"

Lotte then sits beside him. She stares at her shoes. They are old. She wants to hide them.

Lewis breaks the silence. "Okay, look, Lotte. Let's just figure out a time to go and not worry about anything. Money is not even an issue. Let's just go and, and—whatever. I tell you about my boring life, and you can tell me anything or nothing about yours. And thank you—because, because you are—shoot, I'm running off at the mouth. I'm just glad you want to go with me, okay?"

Lotte smiles. Her eyes turn to his. "Thanks for—well, it's just I like to pay my own way and all, but—oh, damn!" She jumps up, breaking the mood. "I just realized I'm supposed to meet somebody in like forty minutes!"

"You need a ride?"

"No, we're meeting at the library. I know, you probably think I'm a nerd."

She heads to her door. But then she turns and says to Lewis, "I'm meeting my boyfriend." She holds the door half open to see his face.

A beat.

"I'm just kidding, Lewis." She shuts the door, smiling coquettishly.

He can hear her laughing in the hallway.

# About the Author

Robert Pacilio was born to teach and to write. He taught high school English for 32 years and was awarded San Diego County's "1998 Teacher of the Year." Since his retirement in 2010, he has spoken at numerous teacher conferences, including the California Teachers Association, about his methods and his curriculum, which are the basis of his young adult novel *Meetings at the Metaphor Café*. He occasionally returns to schools to speak to students about the "invisible things" mentioned in the Metaphor Café.

Mr. Pacilio lives in Encinitas, California with his wife, Pam. His adult children, Nicholas and Anna, are his pride and joy.

His website, www.robertpacilio.com provides information about his speaking engagements and includes reviews of his six novels.

Made in the USA
Coppell, TX
17 February 2026

71619463R00138